The CARE and FEEDING of a PET BLACK HOLE

The CARE and FEEDING of a PET BLACK HOLE

MICHELLE CUEVAS

SIMON & SCHUSTER

First published in Great Britain in 2018 by Simon & Schuster UK Ltd
A CBS COMPANY

Originally published in the USA in 2017 by Dial Books for Young Readers,
an imprint of Penguin Random House

1 3 5 7 9 10 8 6 4 2

Simon & Schuster UK Ltd
1st Floor, 222 Gray's Inn Road
London WC1X 8HB

www.simonandschuster.co.uk
www.simonandschuster.com.au
www.simonandschuster.co.in

Simon & Schuster Australia, Sydney
Simon & Schuster India, New Delhi

A CIP catalogue record for this book
is available from the British Library.

PB ISBN 978-1-4711-7018-8
eBook ISBN 978-1-4711-7019-5

Printed and bound by CPI Group (UK) Ltd, Croydon, CR0 4YY

MIX
Paper from
responsible sources
FSC® C020471

Simon & Schuster UK Ltd are committed to sourcing paper
that is made from wood grown in sustainable forests and support the Forest
Stewardship Council, the leading international forest certification organisation.
Our books displaying the FSC logo are printed on FSC certified paper.

For Eddie, with love

✳

CHAPTER ONE

✳

The Mysterious Something That Followed Me Home

This story began on an afternoon the color of comets, with a girl dressed all in black. A sad girl. A girl with a hole in her heart, and darkness on the horizon.

That girl, of course, was me.

"My name is Stella Rodriguez," I told the guard at the gates to NASA. "I'm eleven years old. I'm here to speak with Carl Sagan."

It was late, almost dark, and I was alone. You and Mom would not have approved.

The guard looked up as if he'd heard an annoying mosquito, decided he imagined it, and went back to reading his magazine.

"Actually," I tried again, "I'm Carl Sagan's great-great-great-great-granddaughter, and I'm here at NASA to tell him that in the future we've invented time travel!"

"Please go away," said the guard.

"But I have an appointment . . ."

"No," said the guard, "you definitely don't."

"*Fine*, okay, maybe I don't!" I said, a bit too loudly. "But if you take into consideration chaos theory or the butterfly effect, the very notion of long-term predictions—for example, an *appointment*—becomes an absurd impossibility. Time—"

But before I could continue trying to sound scholarly, an ear-piercing alarm started ringing. Lights began flashing, and I could hear shouts from inside the building.

"Okay," I said, putting up my hands. "Let's all just take it easy. I'll go peacefully. No need for alarms. I'm too bookish for prison!"

But the guard wasn't paying attention to me. He grabbed his phone and started shouting, something about code reds and protocol, and before I knew what was happening he had run inside, leaving the gate wide open.

I wish I were the type of person who would sneak into NASA during a molecular-robot-alien-rocket-invasion-explosion. But you know very well I'm not that type. Not even close. I'm more of a chicken-liver-jellyfish-fraidy-cat type.

And so I left. I left without seeing Carl Sagan, or giving him the important package I'd come to deliver. Time was of the essence, since the Voyager launch date—August 20, 1977—was mere months away.

Avoiding the alarms at NASA, I went to the bus stop and waited. It was the last moment of light, and I had a strange feeling. Like when you sense a breeze on your ankles in a room with no open windows or doors. Like when you're sure you can see a face in the moon, and it's staring right at you. Like when you're the seeker during hide-and-seek, and you just know you're being watched through a closet keyhole. I darted my eyes from side to side, looking in the bushes and up at the trees. I didn't see anything anywhere but dusk.

And so I was understandably relieved when the bus came around the bend. That is, until I got *on* the bus, and things started to get even stranger, if possible.

"My wallet!" shouted a businesswoman. "Someone stole my wallet!"

Everyone scanned the bus for a shady-looking character.

"And where's my toupee?" asked an elderly man.

This continued for three more stops, shouts of *Where's my lunch?* and *Who took my pet frog?* To get off the bus, I had to weather an obstacle course of people on their hands and knees searching for something-or-other under their seats.

The stop was only a few minutes from home, but it felt like miles. I mean, what was going on?! The dusk had turned to straight-up gloom, which wasn't good because by that point I had a severe case of the creeps, a heebie-jeebie fever, and a touch of the willies. I'm not afraid of the dark—you know that from all our time spent stargazing— but the minute I started walking, I got goose bumps down my arms and legs and all the way up my neck. I had such a case of the jumps that I'm pretty sure I had goose bumps on my eyeballs, which, by the way, were not helping because in a matter of minutes it had gone from almost-dark-outside-gloom to dark-at-the-bottom-of-a-pocket.

I looked from side to side.

"Who's there?" I asked. No one answered. Has anyone in any scary movie ever answered that question? *Oh, glad you asked, it's me the axe murderer. Dang it! That was actually supposed to be a surprise . . .*

So I did what anyone in my position would do. I started to run. Fast. I ran through the dark-like-the-muck-down-a-drain, I sprinted through the dark-as-the-inside-of-a-whale. I didn't hear footsteps or twigs breaking behind me, but the feeling was becoming stronger. Someone was lingering just out of view. I was being watched. I was being followed.

But by who?

Or, worse still . . . by *what?*

CHAPTER TWO

✳

Hello, Darkness

"WHERE HAVE YOU BEEN?! YOU WERE SUP-
POSED TO BE WATCHING ME UNTIL MOM
GETS HOME. I COULD HAVE EATEN GLUE OR
SOMETHING!"

That shrill voice belonged, of course, to Cosmo. A
fitting name given that he's a total space cadet of a five-
year-old brother.

"Shhhhh!" I said. "Help me batten down the hatches
and secure the premises."

I ran around locking doors, closing all the window
shades, and turning off the lights. I peered out through
a crack in the front curtains. It had begun to rain and it

was hard to see whatever monster had been following me home.

"This is fun," whispered a voice behind me. "What are we doing?"

I looked down at Cosmo. He squeezed his little hands in excitement.

"*Did* you eat glue?"

"No," he replied sheepishly.

"Good," I said, "very mature. Come on, I'll make us some dinner."

After fear-flavored grilled cheese sandwiches and tomato soup eaten in almost-dark, I told Cosmo I was going to do my homework, but really I just needed some alone time to think. I put on my fuzzy blue robe with the stars on it, and stared out my bedroom window on the second floor, trying to get a better view of the front yard. I tried using my telescope, but it just made me sad. Extra sad. Sadder than my lingering, everyday fog. It had been our father-daughter thing, just you and me, but now you're gone and there are monsters in the yard and everything is wrong.

I sat slumped with my chin on the windowsill. A raindrop slid down the glass like a tiny shooting star.

"I wish," I said, closing my eyes, "that I could make everything awful just . . . disappear."

When I opened my eyes, I caught a glimpse of something outside, just for a moment, before it darted into a cardboard box near the trash cans on the curb.

"Huh?" I asked. I used my hand to clear the fog from the glass. Yes, there was definitely something in the box, something small, and dark, and shivering. *A kitten*, I thought, trying to convince myself that I had seen the flash of whiskers and flick of a tail.

Armed with rain boots and a flashlight, I made my way outside. Luckily, Cosmo had gone to his room and wasn't around to bug me.

"It's just a cat or a stray dog," I said to myself as I crept across the yard and through the rain.

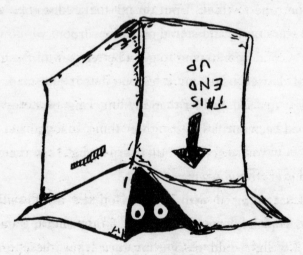

"Here, kitty kitty," I said as I got closer. "Please don't be a skunky skunky."

I moved slowly and carefully, trying to see the critter. But when my flashlight lit up the inside of the box, what I saw was not a kitten or pup. It wasn't even a skunk. What it was was . . . *darkness.*

I stumbled back away from the box, tripped on the curb, and dropped the flashlight. When I finally retrieved it, my hands were shaking as I aimed it back at what I thought I'd seen. The thing inside was gone! I flailed the light around wildly, and found the creature, creeping closer and closer toward me. It didn't seem to have legs or arms. It was just a blob of darkness no bigger than a rabbit—but not regular darkness, no. This was dark like the dark inside an old, closed book— except with two eyes. Eyes that shimmered, and seemed to have tiny galaxies inside of them.

"ACK!" I yelled, pointing at the thing. The thing, in response, looked behind it to see what was so scary.

"Stay back!" I said. But every time I took a step away, the creature crept a little closer to me. In fact, from the way it moved and the look in its eyes, I got the craziest feeling: *I think it wants me to pet it.*

But I'm not insane. Instead, I threw my flashlight at it, hoping it would run away. To my shock, though, the flashlight didn't hit the creature; it just disappeared completely *inside* the thing. The flashlight was there one moment, and gone the next, absorbed without a trace.

"What in the world . . . ?" I asked.

And then, in the dim glow of the streetlamp, the creature gave a very unceremonious, light-filled . . . burp.

CHAPTER THREE

✷

Things I Know About the Thing

You're probably wondering what I did after the creature from the cardboard box swallowed my flashlight, aren't you? Did I run? Call the National Guard? Faint?

Well, I did what I thought *you* would do. I invited it inside, out of the rain.

"So this is my room," I explained. "It's small, but it's home."

I hadn't yet touched the creature. Once I started walking backward toward the house, it just sort of followed me. It didn't seem dangerous, but then again, how would I know? Maybe it was lulling me into a sense of security with those big, needy eyes, and was going to devour me any minute.

The thing had started swallowing stuff in my room—nothing important, just dust bunnies and some of Cosmo's unidentifiable "works of art" that he'd drawn for me. I dumped out a jar of pennies and scattered them around, hoping that would keep the thing busy while I made a list.

Things I Know About the Thing
Very, very dark
No hands or legs, just a blob
Has eyes, I think
The eyes look like little galaxies
~~Swallows~~ ~~Absorbs~~ Disappears anything it wants
Likes to eat flashlights, dust, poorly executed artwork, pennies
Docile (so far)
Seems to want to be touched???

My first thought was *ALIEN*. It's an extraterrestrial being that escaped from NASA and followed me home. But from everything I knew about aliens, they were usually green, had arms and legs, and didn't want to be petted like a puppy.

I pointed to a poster of the Milky Way on my wall.

"Is that your home?" I asked. "Outer space?"

The creature didn't seem to recognize the galaxy as its place of residence or, if it did, was more interested in consuming all of my left shoes one by one.

I looked and looked through all of my science books, trying to find anything that resembled this creature. And then, in a book about theoretical astronomy, I found this:

Black holes form when a massive star dies and collapses into itself. Because of the relationship between mass and gravity, this means they have an extremely powerful gravitational force. Virtually nothing can escape. Even light is trapped by a black hole.

A black hole is a dark center of gravity that swallows everything in its path.

Was that the answer?

Am I, I wondered, *the proud owner of a pet black hole?*

CHAPTER FOUR

✳

The Voyager & The Clawfoot

I didn't have long to contemplate this idea. I heard keys jangling in the door below, and Mom's voice floating up the stairs.

"Bug? Sorry I'm late. Where are you?"

Bug. Mom's special nickname for me since I'd asked for a bug-collecting kit when I was barely old enough to talk. It wasn't my favorite nickname, as I'm sure you remember, but now wasn't the time to quibble.

I scanned the room wildly. There were half-disappeared papers and mismatched shoes on the floor, a chunk was missing from my bedspread, and a black hole was sucking up pennies one by one like Scrooge the Hoover vacuum.

"Just . . . stay here!" I said to the black hole.

"DON'T COME UP TO MY BEDROOM I'M COMING DOWN NO REASON JUST DON'T!" I shouted through my door in a totally (not at all) calm, cool, collected way. I had a hunch that if Mom found out I was entertaining a space phenomenon in my room, she wouldn't approve.

I slammed the door behind me, looked both ways down the hall like a criminal, and went to find Mom in the kitchen, where she was unpacking groceries.

"Oh, there you are," she said. "I thought I heard you screaming."

"Yup," I said, "that was me. Can I help you with anything?"

Ack! The minute the words left my mouth, I worried the jig was up. It was totally out of character for me to offer to help with chores.

"Well," said Mom, "you could watch your brother in the tub. That would be a huge help. Thanks, sweetie."

She kissed the top of my head and walked out. Great. Now I had to spend time with crazy Cosmo.

"STORM NEPTUNIAN WILL BE SO EXCITED!" said Cosmo. He was over the moon when I told him I'd be hanging out during his "bath" tonight instead of Mom. I say "bath" in quotes because, of course, he wears a bathing suit and stays in his "ship" he calls *The Claw-*

foot with his stupid Storm Neptunian doll for hours at a time.

"Do you want to get in with me and Storm?" he asked.

"Cosmo, I will never in a billion-trillion-gazillion years get in the tub with you," I said. "Now just wash your hair and let's go."

Hoping he'd be quiet, I went back to making my list.

<u>Possible Places to Hide a Black Hole</u>
  1. Inside another black hole?

But Storm Neptunian was feeling particularly chatty. Cosmo kept pulling the string on his back to make the doll talk.

"Don't be crabby!" yelled Storm, and: *"Could you be a bit more Pacific?"*

The doll had the voice of a TV meteorologist. *Tonight expect a gale-force front of annoying little brother followed by a high-pressure headache,* I thought.

"Must you?" I asked over my notebook.

Cosmo, of course, ignored my pleas for silence. He pulled Storm's string again.

"Water you doing?" yelled the doll.

"Yes, and how was your day?" asked Cosmo, casually leaning over the side of the claw-foot tub.

"I went to NASA," I said. Great. Another rookie mistake by my black-hole brain.

"The place where you always told Dad you wanted to work?" he asked.

I gave him The Look. The one that said, *We don't talk about Dad, ever, and you know it.*

"Why'd you go there?" he tried instead.

"Because I wanted to drop off a recording," I answered.

"Why?" asked Cosmo.

"Because I wanted Carl Sagan to have it."

"Why?"

"Because he's an amazing astronomer who's launching a spacecraft called the Voyager, and there's a record on board with all the wonderful sounds of Earth."

"Why?"

"Because he wants the aliens to know Earth is friendly and welcoming. The Voyager Golden Record contains all our best sounds—songs and languages, humans and animals—and it will be launched into space like a message in a bottle thrown into the cosmic ocean! It even has the best, most poetic whale song chosen from all the whale songs."

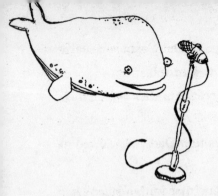

"Why?"

"Because whale songs are beautiful."

"Why?"

"They're sort of haunting and soothing. There are other great sounds too. There's birds, crickets, wind, rain, laughter, kissing, footsteps, tools, a car, a tractor."

"Why?"

"I guess they thought the aliens might want to hear a tractor."

"Why?"

I stared at Cosmo. He'd finally stumped me. Why *would* an alien want to hear a tractor?

Cosmo stopped his one-word interrogation for a moment and looked thoughtful.

"Are there sad sounds too?" he asked.

"What do you mean?" I asked.

"Well, you said laughing and kissing, and those are happy sounds. There's no growling tummies or yelling? No crying?"

"I guess that's probably true," I said, realizing he was right.

"Why?" he asked again.

Because, I wanted to say, *the aliens would turn right*

around in their UFO if they ever knew it was possible for humans to be as sad as I am. If they knew how much I miss you, Dad—how much the feeling follows me around all the time like a stray dog. How most of the time, my own voice sounds like a fake recording of a happy person. How I haven't laughed, not once, since you died.

But I didn't say any of that. Instead, I just reached over and pulled the string on the back of Storm Neptunian.

"I think you're FIN-tastic!"

I didn't feel fintastic. I felt sad, as always. I felt worried. I felt as if I had no idea what on earth I was going to do with the black hole hiding in our house.

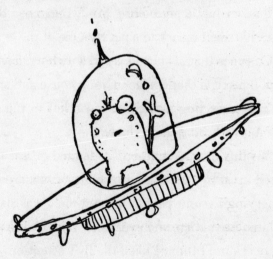

CHAPTER FIVE

✳

A Beginner's Guide to the Care and Feeding of Black Holes

I've never had a pet before. Well, I suppose that's not entirely true. I once had a pet fly. One of those metallic-green types that always looks freshly born from a neon sign. The type that comes in your house and spends its entire life circling a dirty dish you left in the sink and bashing its head against the window.

But this fly was different. It landed on the desk and gazed up at me. That kind of multi-lens stare could be unnerving to some people, but not me. I was six, Cosmo had just been born, and everyone was ooh-ing and ahh-ing over him. I think I liked the fly's attention.

Maybe it was weird to keep a fly as a pet, but if you

think about it, we humans have chosen some wild things as pets. Horses, raccoons, gorillas, I've seen it all. Don't even get me started on pet rocks.

Our entire relationship, mine with the fly, lasted exactly two hours. When the room became stuffy and I opened the window, my fly maneuvered so deftly and swiftly out the window, I began to think his glass-bashing and dizzy-dish-circling had been a trick and a means of escape. Without so much as a good-bye, I watched the metallic-green atom zip away into a dusty sunbeam, never to return.

* * *

"I need every book you have on how to train a puppy," I said.

I was standing in the library, fidgeting nervously. *What was Larry eating in my room right now?* was all I could think about. Larry was the name I'd given it— short for Singularity, which I'd read is a place of infinite gravity at the heart of a black hole. All this, of course, being short for Thing-That-Is-Going-to-Eat-Our-Whole-House-if-I-Don't-Do-Something-and-Fast.

I hadn't even wanted to give him a name. If you name a thing, then you get attached. But he refused to respond to "Hey you," so my hand was forced.

I'd tried other, cooler names.

"How about Nox, or Poe, or Zorro, or Ink?" I'd said.

He'd ignored them all.

"How about . . . Larry?" I asked.

The black hole perked right up.

"Great," I said, rolling my eyes. "Maybe next week we can find a unicorn and name it Steve."

steve

The librarian at the desk was smiling down at me.

"You want some books on dogs?" she asked. "How sweet. What kind of dog do you have?"

"A really hungry one," I replied.

The librarian found me three books: *The Good Dog*

University, *The Art of Raising a Happy Puppy,* and my personal favorite, *Perfect Puppy in Seven Days.* I assumed the entire world would be *gone* in a week if I didn't succeed.

The problem with training a black hole, if you're wondering, is that nobody really knows anything about them. It's all theoretical-this and possibly-perhaps-hypothetical-that.

As I flipped through the dog-training books, I kept reading the same thing: Use positive reinforcement. As in, when the puppy does something right, you give it a treat, like a Milk-Bone. But what would be a treat for a black hole?

It turned out, I was about to get my answer.

"Choke it up!" I shouted at Larry.

I had just arrived home from the library to find one very contented-looking black hole and one very *empty* hamster cage.

"How could you eat him?" I asked. "I mean, he smelled . . . *so bad.*"

Our class had tried everything to de-stink our class pet, Stinky Stu. We cleaned his cage religiously, bathed him, groomed him, we even dabbed him with natural oils and perfumes like a tiny, furry king. Nothing worked.

He still smelled like a scratch-and-sniff of hippo burps. Like a landfill filled with landfill. Like a romantic bouquet of rotten eggs. And now this: I'd been given the soul-breaking task of caring for the rank rodent for the entire school vacation, and I'd already let it get eaten by a black hole. How was I going to explain *that* to my class?

Stinky Stu's little wheel creaked eerily in his cage, but there was nobody left to go for a run. And so, before I could get around to Larry's training, I had to run all the way back to town, to the pet store, and buy a replacement hamster.

After I got home Cosmo discovered me in the kitchen rubbing some gross cheese I'd found in the back of the fridge all over New Stu.

"What are you doing?" asked Cosmo.

"What does it look like I'm doing? I'm trying to stink up this hamster!" I said. My nerves were, obviously, a bit frayed by that point.

"Oh," Cosmo said with a shrug. He grabbed an apple and left. You can always tell a weirdo by the way they don't find weird activities the least bit weird.

When I got upstairs, I put New Stu in Stinky Stu's vacant cage and collapsed on my bed in a puddle of exhaustion.

"Don't take this the wrong way," I said to the black hole, "but you are roughly an infinite amount more work than a pet rock."

Larry had already crept over to New Stu's cage and was staring. His eyes looked just like a toddler's when they see something they want. In fact, they looked a lot like Cosmo's had when he was small and saw something soft and cuddly that he wanted to hug. This gave me an idea for our training. I went and got New Stu out of his woodchip nest and held him a short way from Larry.

"Look how soft he is," I said. "Ooooh. Ahhhh. Don't you just want to snuggle him?"

I stroked New Stu like a game show host showing off a prize. *If you're lucky, you could take home this Brand. New. Hamsterrrrr!* Well, Larry looked like he was about to faint from wanting that hamster so badly. He looked so stricken, I actually started to feel kind of bad.

"Sorry, you can't eat the hamster," I said. "But can you . . . sit?" Larry looked like he was computing, and then, to my surprise, he *did* sit. Well, he flopped lower to the ground and stayed still at least. For a moment, I forgot what I was dealing with, and reached out to give Larry a congratulatory pat. He closed his eyes and leaned in like a purring kitten. But when I touched him, my hand momentarily vanished.

"Ack!" I shouted, jumping back, staring at my hand.

Larry looked sadder than ever, and that's when it struck me: He didn't want to *eat* New Stu. He wanted to cuddle him. Larry had never been touched in his life, not once, never hugged or held. How could he, being a black hole and all? That, I realized, was why he loved soft things so much. He wasn't hungry. He wasn't bad. He just wanted something to *love*.

CHAPTER SIX

✶

The Time Traveler

I don't have many friends. Truth be told, you can take away that *m* because I don't have *any* friends, actually. Cosmo does, because he's five and kids that age just whirl around together on the playground like chaotic galaxies. And Mom does because she's a member of so many clubs—knitting, recipes, falconry, sport fishing. So the only conclusion is this: I inherited my lone wolf tendencies from you. Like father, like daughter, I suppose.

But Larry was different. It didn't particularly matter what I talked about to him. He never replied. And he *liked* me, just like that, without me having to impress him or pretend to care about Magic 8-Ball predictions or a new dance craze. He liked me so much that every night while I slept he would settle down and sleep at the foot of my bed. He was there, every morning, just staring at me like I was the best, most interesting thing in the universe. It felt pretty good. To be honest, it felt a little like you were here again.

I even showed Larry our constellations.

I had lied to Mom when she asked about them a few weeks after we'd said good-bye to you. Every day still felt as if it took place in the underwater level of an arcade game. I told her I'd taken all the constellations down from my ceiling and thrown them away.

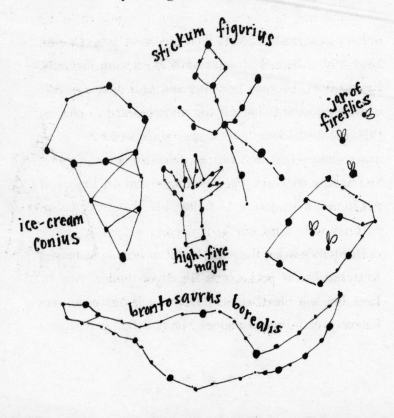

stickum figurius

jar of fireflies

ice-cream conius

high-five major

brontosaurus borealis

But what was I supposed to do?

"Hey Bug," she had said, "I was thinking maybe we could do something together today."

"Something like what?" I'd asked.

"Well, I was thinking," she said, "we could make up some constellations."

The constellations. Yours and mine. You had brought home the packages of glow-in-the-dark stars the first week we moved into this house. We spent hours deciding how to organize them on the ceiling. Should we do the Milky Way? The astrological signs? The winter sky? Fall? Spring?

In the end, of course, we decided to just make up our own constellations. Things like Ice-Cream Conius, High-Five Major, Low-Five Minor, Stickum Figurius, Brontosaurus Borealis, and others we hadn't named yet: the one that looks like a jar of fireflies, the one that looks like a bear in a tiny party hat, and the one that looks like a deer who tried to fly a kite but got the string caught in his antlers. All so majestic, really.

They were ours, our little inside jokes, our tiny memories, the kind that fit so perfectly into your pocket—the kind you find later like a forgotten dollar bill in a jacket you haven't worn since last spring.

So when Mom asked to make up constellations with me, I fibbed. I told her I had taken them all down, thrown them away. I told her I'm too old to be making up constellations.

But they were still there. Invisible, blending in with the paint on the ceiling during the day, only coming out at night when I was in bed all alone. But now I had Larry, so I showed him our best constellation.

"This one," I told Larry, "is my favorite. It's called the Time Traveler. Allow me to explain. You see, some of the starlight in the night sky has taken years to reach us from the star it left."

Larry looked, I admit, a tad confused.

"Okay," I tried again. "So light travels at about 670 million miles per hour, which since you can't drive, I'll just tell you is super-fast. Stars are so far away that even light from the closest star to Earth, named Proxima Centauri, is 4.24 light-years away from us. Do you understand what that means? It means it takes 4.24 years

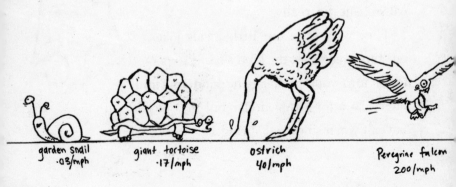

garden snail
.03/mph

giant tortoise
.17/mph

ostrich
40/mph

Peregrine falcon
200/mph

from when light leaves Proxima until it reaches our eyes. Some are way farther away. One of the most distant stars we can see without a telescope is Deneb in the constellation Cygnus, which is almost three thousand light-  years away. The light we see from Deneb started its journey to us when ancient Rome was just a few houses with thatched roofs."

Larry's eyes seemed to widen with wonder.

"Think about it," I said. "By the time we actually see a star, in the years it has taken the light to reach us, that star might be dead, might have totally exploded. What I'm saying is, the world is full of dum-dums standing around making wishes on stars that might not even exist anymore!"

I could almost see laughter in Larry's eyes.

Starlight
670, 616, 629/mph

"So my dad and I decided to make a constellation of stars from all different distances. Some might still be around. Some might be gone. The night sky isn't a single moment in the universe; it's a patchwork of time. That's what my dad used to say. That's how we came up with the name: the Time Traveler. I always thought it looked a bit like me."

Larry gazed up, entranced.

I wanted to hug him then, to cuddle him like a real pet. But I couldn't. I knew what would happen—that my hand, my head, and then my whole self would disappear inside.

So instead I wondered what I would do if I could time travel. Where I would go. I think the answer is probably pretty obvious, but what would I say to you if given another chance? I wasn't sure. *I guess*, I thought as I floated off to sleep, *I'd start with a real humdinger of a joke* . . .

CHAPTER SEVEN

✳

Think Like a Proton

Larry and I became so close, I even told him what was on the recording, the one I was trying to deliver to NASA the day he decided to follow me home.

I told him about Carl Sagan the astronomer, and NASA and how they were building a spacecraft called the Voyager. I told him what I'd told Cosmo, about how on the Voyager there would be a Golden Record, and how the record would contain everything on Earth.

"You have to wonder," I told Larry, "how other kids at school are able to stay so focused on the length of their pants and movie stars' various chins when things like this are happening in the world."

I showed Larry my list. During classes at school I

wrote and rewrote the lists of everything that would be on the Golden Record. I had them memorized, just about. My favorite was the list of sounds.

1. Music of the Spheres
2. Volcanoes, Earthquake, Thunder
3. Wind, Rain, Surf
4. Crickets, Frogs
5. Birds, Hyena, Elephant
6. Chimpanzee
7. Wild Dog
8. Fire, Speech
9. Tractor
10. Horse
11. Train
12. Auto, Bus
13. Kiss, Mother and Child
14. Footsteps
15. Heartbeat
16. Laughter

I wondered how they decided who got to make the sounds—whose footsteps, whose kiss, whose heartbeat, and laughter, and barking dog would get to be the ones to greet alien life? It was something to think about.

"So I decided to record my dad's laugh," I told Larry.

"And then I planned to go and convince Carl Sagan to put it on the Voyager Golden Record."

I asked Larry if he wanted to hear the recording, and he blobbed his head up and down. It was a good recording. A good memory. But every time I listened to it, it felt as if some giant, invisible thing had come and left footprints in the snow, and inside my chest.

Still, I looked down at the recorder and pressed PLAY.

We'd been sitting at the kitchen table, you and me, with the tape recorder recording.

"Now here's a good one," you said. "How do you organize a space party?"

"I don't know," I said. "How?"

"You *planet*," you replied with a slight smile.

"Plan it. Good one," I said. "I've got one too. Where do geneticists like to swim?"

"Where?" you asked.

"In the gene pool," I said.

"Ha! I like that one," you said. "Hey, by the way, have you heard about the new book about anti-gravity?"

"What about it?" I asked.

"It's impossible to put down," you replied.

And we laughed.

"How do you think like a proton?" I asked.

"How?"

"You stay positive." I giggled.

That one you especially liked. Big laugh for the proton.

"Why are chemists great at solving problems?" I asked.

"I don't know. Why?"

"Because they have all the solutions!"

You laughed, then said, "Why can you never trust atoms?"

"Why?" I asked.

"Because they make up everything!" you replied.

We laughed even harder.

"So," you said, "I guess you got your recording. I'm glad."

"It's definitely a big responsibility."

"Oh, I agree," you agreed. "I mean, you choose someone with one of those high-pitched screaming laughs, and maybe the aliens turn around. If they put some weird snort-laugh on the Voyager record, we can say buh-bye to hovercraft cars and magical space cheese. So long secrets of the galaxy!"

I pressed the STOP button on the recording. Larry looked sad, but that was it. It was the only recording I had of your voice. I wondered if I could rearrange the words on the tape, every noun and verb and adjective, to make a new conversation. But no. We would never speak again, and that truth was one of the many things I wished I could throw away forever into my pet black hole.

CHAPTER EIGHT

✳

My Very Good, Very Bad
Black Hole

And so that's why, after all our bonding, I felt miserable when I yelled at Larry and he ran away and started eating the entire world. But I'm getting ahead of myself.

First, there was the training.

Once I'd figured out that Larry loved furry, fuzzy things, and started using New Stu as a reward, the training went smoothly. Or as smoothly as possible with an unpredictable black hole as my trainee.

"We'll begin by practicing 'sit,'" I explained. "You've done it once, so it should be simple."

Except it actually wasn't simple, because Larry preferred to follow me around like a second shadow. So we moved on to other commands, and those went slightly better. He liked "come," of course, and "heel." "Lie down" took a lot of time—with me sprawled out on the ground like roadkill with Larry beside me—and "roll over" made us both laugh (at least I like to think Larry laughed . . . on the inside). "Shake" was never going to happen on account of Larry's lack of arms and legs, so we moved on to what I knew would be the hardest command of all: the dreaded *"stay."*

This, it seemed, was Larry's downfall. His destroyer and his defeat. He would get this very serious look in his eyes, something similar to a furrowed brow if he'd had one, and he'd *try* to stay. But it was as if the entire world was against him. As if the universe was yelling, *You are Infinite Time and Space! You were born from the Death of a Massive Star! Do not listen to the commands of this Tiny Earthling!*

And so, Larry would stay for about ten seconds, and then the planetary forces would align and compel him across the room to eat a deck of playing cards or an eraser shaped like a hamburger, or just to stand unnervingly close to me for no reason at all.

Which was disappointing because "stay" was the only command I truly needed Larry to learn. "Stay" was, for example, what I needed to say when Larry ate my favorite photo of you.

But I didn't ask him to stay.

Instead I yelled. Loudly.

"How *could* you?!" I screamed. "That was a photo of my dad. I can't replace it. He's gone, and now so is the picture, and it's *all your fault!*"

Larry shrank back against the wall and tried to make himself very, very tiny.

"You're the worst!" I shouted. "I wish you were gone. I wish you'd just *disappear!*"

My anger shook the room, and practically the whole house. Larry couldn't take it, and before I knew what had happened, he had slipped by me and out the door.

"Good! Go!" I yelled. I sat down on the bed with my head in my hands. The photo! It was the one of you holding the telescope I'd picked out for your birthday. I had agonized over that decision for months. I had looked at every magazine a hundred times, and gone back to the store over and over. I snapped the photo the moment you finished unwrapping and saw the surprise inside.

"Wait," I said now, suddenly realizing what I had done. "Oh no, oh no, oh no . . ."

I ran out of the room, down the stairs, and tore through the kitchen and pantry.

"Larry!" I shouted. I sprinted into the bathroom, the bedroom, and the basement. I checked every closet and under every piece of furniture. I even looked in the washing machine and the toilet.

But once I saw the open window in the living room, I knew:

There was a half-trained black hole on the loose in my neighborhood.

CHAPTER NINE

*

The Black Hole Who Ran Away

But how do you find a missing, frightened black hole? I put on my deerstalker hat, the one you bought me during my Sherlock Holmes phase, and tried to think.

"If I were a black hole, where would I go?" I asked myself.

"If *I* were a black hole, I would go to a waterfall and sit under it and drink all the water until I became a portable pool, and then I'd go to the zoo, and I'd save all the whales and penguins and dolphins."

"Do you mind?" I said to Cosmo, who was lingering in the doorway. "This is a private conversation between me and myself."

"I wouldn't save the sea lions, though," he added. "I find them very judgmental."

Cosmo then came into the room uninvited and handed me a pipe. It was shaped like one Sherlock Holmes would use, except bright purple and able to blow bubbles.

"It helps me think," explained Cosmo. "Go ahead."

I shrugged, lifted the pipe, and sighed my frustration into it. Several bubbles floated up, across the room, and out the window.

As they did, a siren started blaring in the distance.

"Smoke detector," said Cosmo, pointing to the pipe.

"No," I said, getting up and running to the front door. "It's a police siren. And I'm pretty sure I know why."

I followed the noise down the street, with Cosmo behind me even after I told him to scram. We hid in the bushes to eavesdrop on a police officer. He was standing outside Mrs. Nimbus's house. She was in her robe, her curlers bopping around her head like tiny pink thoughts trying desperately to escape.

"My gnomes!" she was shouting. "Someone has stolen my garden gnomes!"

"And how many of these gnomes were stolen?" asked the officer.

"One hundred and forty-seven," replied Mrs. Nimbus.

The officer wrote this down.

"And the function and value of these gnomes?"

"Spiritual!" shouted Mrs. Nimbus. "Metaphysical! Priceless!"

"Okay, well, I have the report, and we'll start questioning the neighbors . . ."

The officer turned to leave, but Mrs. Nimbus grabbed his arm.

"Wait!" she shouted. "I haven't given you all their names."

"Of the neighbors?" asked the officer.

"No," said Mrs. Nimbus. "Of the one hundred and forty-seven gnomes. There's Bimphy," she started. "And Dafoodle. Fudgewick. Loopglynn. Zoomwinkle. Nickelbells. Pimpert . . ."

We left long before she finished. Mrs. Nimbus was a widow now, but she and her husband had bought all the gnomes back when they traveled together. She told everyone in the neighborhood about them if they got close enough to listen. Nobody wanted to get stuck talking to Mrs. Nimbus.

Cosmo and I moved on down the street.

This all made me think about my newfound superpower. I guess I forgot to tell you about that. It started when you got sick. And then after you were gone, there it was, full power. It was as if I'd been given infrared night-vision goggles. You see, it turns out there's this whole other parallel universe, right here in this one. And I couldn't see it before, but now I could.

What I mean is, I could see that Mrs. Nimbus wasn't just crazy, but that she was sad. She told her gnome stories because she missed her husband. I had heard her stories about a million times, and I used to hate those boring stories. But now . . . I can't explain it. Now they reminded me of *me*, and how I felt about *our* memories. Before, I couldn't see her. But now I could.

Get what I mean? Total superpower.

"Keep your eyes peeled," I told Cosmo as we walked the neighborhood. "For anything unusual. Anything out of the ordinary. Anything that would make you say—"

"Wowee zowee, look at that!" shouted Cosmo.

"Exactly," I said.

He tugged my arm and pointed.

At every house down the street, the mailboxes had been stolen from their posts. There were also missing yard games, toys, and hibachi grills. Our neighbors were standing on their lawns in a tizzy, and nobody seemed to have seen anything at all.

"The aliens have come!" said an alarmed man to his neighbor. "And they want our hibachi grills!"

"Look," I said, pointing to the ground where his grill had gone missing. There was a distinct trail of cat prints leading away through the bushes.

"Exactly as I suspected," said Cosmo. "The thief is a cat."

I considered explaining my thought process to Cosmo—that the thief was actually *following* a cat because he liked to eat furry animals—but decided better of it.

"Cosmo, could you do me a favor? Could you go home and—"

"Get some milk?" asked Cosmo.

"Milk?" I asked, worried about the answer.

"To lure the cat thief," said Cosmo.

"Of course," I said. "Uh, great idea."

"I'm on it!" said Cosmo. He set off toward home with a giant grin, singing a song about catching a cat. Such a weirdo. Though who was I to talk? I was following cat tracks to find a black hole.

I heard more sirens in the distance. People yelling. Babies crying.

The world, it seemed, was coming to an end. And it was all my fault.

CHAPTER TEN

✶

The Black Hole Who
Ate the World

People are always saying, "Oh, it's not the end of the world." They say it when it rains at a wedding, or if someone sits in a puddle, or that time in fourth grade when I wore the exact same shirt as the teacher on class photo day.

However, if someone said, "My pet black hole is on the loose and eating the planet," someone else would probably say, "Well yes, that does sound like the *actual* end of the world."

But how would it go, this black hole apocalypse?

As I walked down my street looking for Larry, I began to think that *any* black hole would start with this neighborhood. All the colorful houses and cotton-candy hedges and pixie-stick swing sets and boring, endless days.

As I passed a field, I wondered: *What if the black hole eats every cicada and buzzing cricket and chirping frog until they're all gone, every last one?*

And then I'd say to Cosmo, "Do you remember what it was like to stand in the middle of a meadow at dawn and hear the cicadas?"

And Cosmo would say, "What the heck is a cicada?" He'd never know. And I couldn't tell him, because at that point, I wouldn't remember either. Was it a plant? An animal? A teen pop star? A law, a vessel, a cycle of seasons?

Other things would go as well. A kid at school might try to say some common cliché one day, something like, "The dog ate my homework." Except the black hole would have *swallowed up* all the dogs, so he'd be left saying, "The _____ ate my homework."

"The *what?*" the teacher would ask.

"The _____! The _____!" the student would shout, but nothing would come out of his mouth because that word would be gone. Doggone. Poof. And our teacher would think a narwhal had eaten someone's math assignment.

Soon newspaper headlines would read:

EXTRA! EXTRA! THE NEW MUSEUM OF _____ OPENS TODAY!

or

BEWARE! HERDS OF WILD _____ HAVE ESCAPED FROM THE ZOO!

I pictured Mom, just sitting there during breakfast, scratching her head at the newspaper, wondering if they meant a Museum of Pastas (exciting!) or a Museum of Used Gum (not as exciting). Maybe the zoo had lost a herd of hungry lions (yikes!) or a herd of adorable baby ducks (yes, please!). She'd never know!

And what about people? If a black hole swallowed someone, would it be just as if they had died? Or would they be totally wiped away, every memory, as if they had never even existed?

It sounded sad, until I realized that I've been living the alternative to it. The alternative is that someone I love is gone, but I still remember all the little things, and all the big things, and these memories take up all the space in the room.

I remember how you would nonchalantly lean down and tie my shoelace, and how you would dance horribly to a record, and the way you burned dinner whenever you cooked. I remember certain smiles, and smells, and the soft, static sound of the radio when we would listen to a baseball game in the garage. If the black hole could eat those memories, maybe I'd start to feel better.

I always thought the time I'd miss you most was when something sad happened, and you weren't around to comfort me. But it turns out, it's just the opposite. I miss you most when something good happens, and I can't run home and tell you, and I can't see how happy it makes you. Something as big as a scientific discovery I read about in a magazine, or as small as a joke I heard in the cafeteria at school. When I thought of a new constellation the other day, I felt happy for a moment, and then the happiness just disappeared. *Dad would have loved this*, I thought, and BAM, the happy disappeared into that black hole eating the world.

So maybe it wasn't such a tragedy.

Maybe feeling nothing *would* be better than all this.

CHAPTER ELEVEN

✳

Chapter Eleven has been eaten by a black hole.
Please proceed to Chapter Twelve.

CHAPTER TWELVE

✴

The Black Hole Who Came Home

But the world did not end.

I was walking home, head hung low, still imagining Larry taking over cities and towns like a Godzilla garbage disposal, when I saw . . . well, I guess it could only be described as a small gang of hummingbirds. Which was odd, because hummingbirds never seemed like the group type, not like bees or geese. In fact, I'd only ever seen a hummingbird on its own, and even then, it hadn't seemed to want to be seen.

So it was odd that about two dozen would be swarming around the photo booth outside the arcade.

I crept closer, drawn in by the little glowing green birds. I was completely entranced until I heard the metallic whirr of the machine. The curtain was drawn, and I wondered who was inside. I looked down at the opening as the strip of photos slid out.

"Larry!" I shouted, shoving the photo curtain aside. "It's you!"

Larry turned. He looked around the photo booth as if he wanted to find an escape hatch and run.

"It's okay," I said, "I'm not mad anymore. I'm just glad you're okay. I missed you, really I did," I coaxed. "You're a very good black hole, best I've ever met, in fact. Come on, let's go home, whatta ya say?"

And so, Larry started to follow me. I noticed he had grown bigger, almost the size of a Great Dane. He bobbed and weaved, trying to dodge the feisty hummingbirds. Totally fed up, he tried to increase his speed and escape them. No luck. He was like a cartoon character that had bonked his head and now had a permanent halo of tweety birds.

"Larry," I said. "Did you by any chance eat our neighbor's hummingbird feeder?"

Once we arrived home I was able to distract the birds with some sugar water and sneak Larry back to my room. I closed the door behind me, leaned against it, and let out a sigh. I heard steps in the hall, and then a soft knock on my door.

"Bug, honey, it's me," said Mom. "I thought I heard you come in. I don't want to bother you, but your aunt Celeste is coming to dinner and I think she'd really love it if you wore that sweater that she knitted for your birthday. Okeedokee. I need to run to the store. Your brother stole all the milk from the fridge for some reason."

Ack! An Aunt Celeste sighting. And worse, a wearing of one of her dreaded sweaters.

It's hard to even describe an Aunt Celeste sweater. Imagine, if you will, what it would be like to wear a haunted house. There were always strange pockets you'd find on the inside of the neck, or an extra append-age hole, or a weird armpit zipper. The texture was like she was Cinderella and little birds had helped her make the garments, except they weren't cartoon birds, they were actual birds, and they built the sweaters like a nest out of twigs and sticks and mud. And somehow when you wore one, you were always dripping with sweat, but every so often, you'd feel a draft, as if you were trapped in a room on a ninety-degree summer day with one small, oscillating fan. But I'm sure you remember. She used to make sweaters for you too.

I went to my closet and unearthed my collection of Celeste sweaters, dumping them in a pile on the floor. Larry came over to investigate the situation with me. "This one," I said, holding up a sweater that looked like a sheep at a disco, "is from Christmas three years ago. It actually gave me paper cuts. How is that even possible from a sweater?"

Larry, unsurprisingly, was entranced by the fuzzy, furry eyesore.

"Here," I said, holding it out to him. "You want it?"

He paused with delight, and do you know what he did next? If you guessed "ate the monstrosity of a sweater," you would be correct. If you guessed "ate *all* the sweaters as I fed them to him one by one," you'd be even *more* correct. And if you guessed I fell into a blissful sleep that night thinking, *Maybe I was wrong about Larry being trouble; maybe I actually won the pet lottery,* you'd be the most correct of all.

✳

CHAPTER THIRTEEN

The Black Hole Who Disposed of My Problems

"What do you mean ALL YOUR SWEATERS ARE MISSING?"

Mom was, obviously, alarmed at this sweater development.

"I don't know," I said, putting up my hands as if I were the victim. "I went to the closet and they were just . . . *gone*. Poof. It's just so very odd."

"Cosmo, do you know anything about this?" asked Mom.

Cosmo took out his bubble pipe and a small notebook.

"Probably the same cat who stole the garden gnomes and hibachi grills."

My mother shot me one of her desperate *Can you*

translate that from Cosmo to Human? looks. I shrugged my shoulders. It was good that something was keeping their minds occupied and off sweaters and black holes.

And so that night, that glorious night when Aunt Celeste arrived, I was wearing a soft, normal T-shirt made of cotton with only two armholes.

"It's the strangest thing . . ." said Mom. She led her sister into the kitchen for tea and the tale of the missing sweaters.

"Hey guys, my sweater just made a weird noise," said Cosmo, though nobody seemed to be listening. "Almost like the sound of a creaking door . . . and I think I heard a child's laughter . . . *Guys?*"

This was amazing! If I could have high-fived Larry, I would have. It was a revolution. A mutiny. A transformation. I'd gotten rid of the sweaters without having to actually do anything wrong. A natural interstellar phenomenon had eaten them. It was the greatest rule-breaking loophole of our time, and it was all mine.

I decided to experiment. First came the Brussels sprouts. I still don't understand what they even are—cabbages grown on an ant farm? Bite-sized troll boogers? Shrunken Martian heads? Who knows, but I didn't want to eat any of them. Mom knew this, and would notice if she found my portion in the trash. But that night the sprouts weren't in the trash *or* my stomach. They were (hurray!) meteors showering through the endless dark of a black hole.

I did the same later that night when Mom told me it was my turn to take out the trash. The lawn between our house and the curb was a minefield of snails and slugs after dark. *So just wear shoes,* you're probably thinking. *What's the big deal?* I say to you, go step on a snail's shell or find a slug stuck to your sole, then get back to me. I'm sure you'd also choose to feed the trash bags, one by one, to your new composting friend named Larry. I also threw away summer reading assignments I was dreading and my embarrassing diary.

Next I moved on to Cosmo's room. I started with

Storm Neptunian. Cosmo had a million toys, and if I got rid of this ridiculous talking doll, maybe I'd never have to hear that horrendous voice ever again. Into the black hole he went.

"Farewell, Storm Neptunian," I said.

"You've got to be squidding meeeeeeeee," he said in reply, his automated voice disappearing into the darkness.

And finally, I dealt with one of the biggest ongoing annoyances in my life: Cosmo's horrific taste in music. I won't try to describe it. I'll just say that the only band he owned records by was a kids' group called The Fuzzles. Their "hits" included "Stairway to Seven" about a broken elevator, "Heard It Through the Bovine" about a gossiping cow, and "Fartbreak Hotel," which does not, I believe, need any explanation.

Cosmo listened to the records day and night, the volume turned full blast, so I had to wait until he was

taking his bath to sneak in and steal them.

I know, I know, the poor kid. How could I play Frisbee with Larry using my dear brother's beloved records? In my defense, I say to you, listen to "Raindrops Keep Falling on My Undead" (about zombies caught without umbrellas) four thousand times, *then* tell me what you would do, okay?

CHAPTER FOURTEEN

✳

The Black Hole Who Consumed
My Broken Heart

That night, lying in bed and looking up at the constellations on my ceiling, I thought again about how the world was almost swallowed by a black hole. For a moment, the idea seemed almost wonderful. Sure, some good things would disappear, but so would the bad. Right then I wanted to not only be rid of the glowing stars on my ceiling, but also the whole *memory* of them, the whole knowledge that they ever existed.

I mean, sure, a pet black hole is good for disappearing absurd vegetables and haunted sweaters, but what about the other stuff? The stuff that's stuck to your life like ceiling stars? There's no way, for example, to get rid of the memory of you and me as we created constellations on the ceiling. And that memory made me sad. And I didn't want to be sad anymore.

Maybe all I could do was get rid of the *reminders* of the memories. Maybe, over time, there would be nothing left to make me sad. It was worth a try.

I found a box and made my way through the house in the dark, room by room, collecting all the things that reminded me of you, and made me feel as if there was a hole inside my chest. I put the rock polisher inside, the one we'd bought at a tag sale, along with the headlamp I used for late-night explorations with you. I added the chemistry set and the cracked beaker from the Explosion Incident of 1975. I rolled up the poster we'd made together of the periodic table, along with my bug collection, my model of the human brain, and a book about all the astronauts. I even included your hat, the red one with *NASA* on the front.

I threw in the model of our make-believe planet. Technically, that one had not just been ours, but a project we'd made to help me become a member of the Test Tubes, the science club at school. I hadn't gone to any meet-ups in a while. Nobody ever talked to me anyway.

We'd worked on that planet for weeks, named all

the mountains and plains and volcanoes. We'd attached model moons in the correct orbital paths, and even given the whole thing a name. *Stellarium.* It was impressive, but it had to go.

Finally, I put one last thing in the pile. At the top of the heap I placed the recording of your laugh that I'd tried to get on the Voyager Golden Record.

Once I had filled the box, I brought it upstairs to Larry, who was snoozing like a mud puddle at the foot of my bed.

"Hey Larry," I said, "how about a little midnight snack?"

Larry, the chowhound that he was, was happy to oblige. And so I fed him . . .

> One rock polisher
> One headlamp
> One chemistry set
> Several beakers
> My periodic table poster
> My bug collection
> A human brain
> An astronaut book
> Your old red hat
> The Planet of Stellarium
> And a Partridge in a Pear Tree

Larry fetched each, and did not return them.

Finally, there was only one thing left in the dark bottom of the box: the recording of your laugh. I took it out, the small tape recorder with those simple buttons—RECORD, PLAY, and STOP. I didn't want to hear it again. It would just make me question my decision. But when I held it out to Larry he paused. He looked at me. He seemed to be saying *Are you sure about this one?*

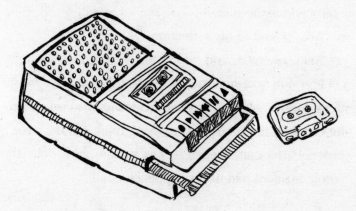

But I did not pause. Or stop. I wanted to put the recording—and all my memories, for that matter—into the nothingness, so that I could just feel . . . well, nothing.

Finally I was able to coax Larry to eat the recording by putting it inside my new left shoe.

Afterward, when I got back into bed, I tried to figure out whether things had changed. Did I feel different now? Happy maybe, or even free?

I reached up and absentmindedly touched the side of my chin, the place with the scar caused by the Great Beaker Explosion Incident of 1975. Strange. Normally, I could feel the moon-shaped scar when I ran my fingers along the skin. But now . . .

Nothing.

I got up, turned on all the lights, and moved to the mirror. I studied my face, turned it at an angle, and searched for the scar.

"Ack!" I said to my reflection.

"Ack!" my reflection said to me.

The skin was smooth and perfect. No scar. It was as if we'd never decided to make a volcano in a beaker. Perfect, as if I'd never added the wrong liquids in the wrong order. Perfect, as if once it was in the black hole, the whole incident had never happened at all.

CHAPTER FIFTEEN

*

The Black Hole Who
Swallowed a Bug

The next morning Mom was acting very odd. I wondered if it was somehow connected to all the memories I'd fed to Larry the night before.

First, she came to make sure I was awake. On a Sunday.

"Stella," she said, tapping on my door. "Are you coming down for breakfast?"

"Whaaaa?" I groaned. "Is our house on fire?"

"We're having breakfast now," she continued, a manic glee in her voice. "You should come down. I'll wake Cosmo too."

I slowly rubbed the sleep from my eyes and brain, and hauled myself out of bed one foot at a time. *What is going on?* I wondered as I made my way down the stairs. Something was strange, but I couldn't quite put my finger on it.

When I got to the kitchen, Mom was sitting at the table, grinning like I hadn't seen her grin in a very long time.

"Hey, Mom . . ." I said, sitting down. "Is there a gas leak or something? You seem kind of weird."

"I'm not weird," said Mom playfully. "I've just got a surprise for you."

"Okay . . ."

Mom took my hand in hers. "Stella, I know things have been hard, for all of us. And I want you to know I'm proud of you, for being brave, for just being you, and for everything."

"Mom," I said.

"Yes, Stella?"

"You . . . you called me Stella."

"Well, yes." She laughed. "That's your name. What else would I call you?"

Bug, I thought, *you'd call me Bug.* But then I remembered the bug collection I'd thrown inside Larry. What if somehow, some way, making the bugs disappear had made Mom forget I ever had a nickname in the first place?

Uh-oh.

"Anyhow, silly," she went on, "I wanted to do something for you. Then I noticed your puppy-training books the other day, and I thought, *Well, hmmm, maybe*. It's a big responsibility—"

"Mom, no, you didn't—"

But before I could finish, Cosmo came bursting into the room wearing his footie pajamas, his hair standing on end.

"You guys!" he shouted, waving around a framed photo. "This photo of Dad and me at the baseball game! His hat is gone! His red hat, he was wearing it in the photo. And now he's not!"

"Okay, honeybun, that's a fun game," said Mom, pulling Cosmo onto her lap and putting the photo aside. "But listen, I was just telling your sister I saw her puppy-training books, and I got you both a surprise."

"Wait, what did you say about a red hat? The NASA one?" I asked Cosmo.

"Okay, I'll get it then," said Mom, trying to stay chipper even though her children were clearly ignoring her.

Cosmo handed me the photograph. I stared. I couldn't believe it. Cosmo was right. The hat was gone from the picture. The very hat I had thrown into a black hole the night before . . .

"Surprise!" said Mom. She had opened the kitchen door and was holding a box with holes all over it.

"Neat box!" said Cosmo.

"Thank you, dear. But the box is not the surprise. Open it," said Mom.

So we did, even though I already knew what was inside. A disaster, that's what.

A misfortune.

An undoing.

A calamity.

"A DOG!" shouted Cosmo.

CHAPTER SIXTEEN

✳

A Dog of No Name

"But why did you have to get a dog who's so fluffy?" I asked. "So soft, and furry, and easily digestible . . ."

Nobody was listening. Why would they? There was a majorly distracting, fluffy, soft, furry, easily digestible puppy in the room.

Mom decided the puppy would sleep in my room. If I'd learned anything from my training books, it was that you had to be firm, with dogs or black holes. The puppy—who I had yet to name for fear that it would just create attachment to an animal that might be eaten— would sleep in her crate on the floor, and Larry would stay on the bed. I explained this setup to both of them at length, but five minutes after I turned out the lights that first night, the puppy was crying like crazy and Larry had slinked out of bed.

"Stop. Right. There," I said to Larry. "I know she's soft, but you are *not* allowed to touch the dog. And by touch her, I do mean eat her."

Larry flopped to the ground, disheartened.

"New plan. Puppy in bed, Larry on the floor."

This helped with the crying, but every time I started to drift to sleep, I sensed a presence, and sure enough when I opened my eyes, there was Larry, trying to act all innocent as if he wasn't planning to devour-by-cuddling the furry thing in my bed.

That entire night I got, maybe, twelve minutes of sleep.

"You look tired," said Cosmo at breakfast. "Did the dog keep you awake? Ha. 'Dog.' Shouldn't we give her a name?"

I was tired and cranky. And still worried about getting attached to something that wasn't long for this world. "No name," I said.

Cosmo looked off dramatically into the distance. "A Dog of No Name," he said, waving his hand in the air as if he was spelling out the words.

"Sounds good," I said, closing my eyes and resting my head on the table. I could hear the puppy upstairs, whining outside my bedroom door, begging to be let inside and become Larry's lunch.

✳ ✳ ✳

What I soon learned was that my two pets were actually quite different. One was a space phenomenon, and the other, a dog. One intrigued astronomers and astrophysicists with its mysterious inner workings. The other was slightly cross-eyed and never stopped licking things. One had been trained using a hamster. The other was, I feared, going to be about as easy to tame as the wind and the rain.

"Sit," I would say to A Dog of No Name, offering up a treat. "Roll over. Come. Lie down. Stay."

With each command, the puppy would just turn her head to one side, then the other, then back again, as if a different angle would cause my gibberish to make sense to her tiny brain.

And of course, since he followed us around like a shadow, Larry would hear my commands and think I was talking to him. Out of the corner of my eye I would see him sitting, rolling over, coming toward me, lying down, and staying put.

Hmmmm, I finally thought. *Maybe I could use this.*

I sat the dog on one side of the room and took Larry to the other.

"Larry," I said. "Lie down."

Larry, ever the well-trained black hole, spilled himself across the floor.

"Good," I said. "Now roll over."

Larry rolled his darkness across the floor, accidentally absorbing a pair of smelly socks but otherwise in perfect form. I walked across the room.

"Larry, come."

He did as he was told. The dog watched as we did the tricks over and over and over again. Somewhere in the outer reaches of space that were her puppy brain, a moment, a spark, a comet streaked across her mind. Because when I again told Larry to sit, the dog watched the black hole, walked up beside him, and actually mimicked the sitting. Maybe it was the joy of having a new friend, but Larry didn't try to touch the puppy or eat it at all.

In fact, for the next few days, the two were inseparable. They window-gazed near each other, slept near each other, and played with each other. They could have rivaled Batman and Robin (if the goal of comic book heroes was to eat everything in your house, then periodically poo on the rug). If they'd been on TV they would have had their own theme song:

> *They can solve any crime,*
> *they can reach any goal!*
> *They're the bestest of friends:*
> *Dog and Sidekick Black Hole!*

CHAPTER SEVENTEEN

✶

The Black Hole Who Devoured My Reality

I thought that everything was going great. I thought, *Hey, I trained a black hole AND an untrainable puppy! I can do anything!*

And why did I think these things, you ask?

Because I'm a fool, that's why.

And why am I a fool?

Because while I'd been distracted by A Dog of No Name, I hadn't noticed the few orange leaves on the trees. I thought it was summer still, but it was almost autumn, and my world had been quietly, softly, in a whispered voice, falling apart all around me.

I'm no expert in the physics of memories eaten by black holes, but there had definitely been signs. The scar on my chin. The nickname. The photo with the red hat. Why hadn't I taken it all more seriously?

One day I had to think and think before I remembered my nickname. Once I remembered, I wrote it down. I started writing *everything* down, partly out of good science, and partly because I thought I might be going crazy.

Stranger things began to occur. I heard there was going to be a science competition for all the local schools this coming year, but when I called Tony Luna from the Test Tubes, he acted as if he didn't even know me.

"Hi Tony, it's Stella," I said into the phone.

"Stella who?" he asked.

"Stella Rodriguez," I replied, feeling warmth in my cheeks. "Look, I know I've missed a lot of meetings, but I was curious what you guys are thinking for the science fair this year. I had this interesting idea about black holes, actually, and—"

But Tony cut me off.

"Stella? From school?"

"Yes, Stella! From school and the Test Tubes, obviously."

"Stella . . ." continued Tony. "I don't know if this is a prank or something, but you've never come to a Tubes meeting. You've never joined."

"What are you talking about?" I asked. "I joined last

year. I made a planet with my dad and . . . it was called the Planet of . . . of . . ."

But as hard as I tried, I couldn't remember the name.

"Sorry to bother you," I said, hanging up the phone abruptly, my voice shaking.

I went to my notebook and looked back at the list of things I'd fed to Larry.

The Planet of Stellarium

So if the planet never existed, then I never joined the science club? I guess that would explain why Tony was acting so strange.

Later that evening, I walked by the bathroom. Cosmo was, as usual, sitting in the tub. But instead of playing, he was just sitting there, staring at a shampoo bottle.

"What are you doing?" I asked.

"Just reading these ingredients," he said. He wasn't wearing his goggles or snorkel or fins. He didn't ask me, like he did every bath, to get in and play scuba games with him.

"You're not going to play anything?" I asked.

"What would I play?" he asked.

"What about Storm Neptunian?" I suggested.

"Storm who?" asked Cosmo.

Shampoo

But of course, I knew in an instant what had happened. Cosmo had been given his talking Storm Neptunian for his birthday, and it was the reason he started watching the show and learning the songs and wearing goggles and snorkels and fins in the tub.

"You know," I said, trying to jog his memory.

"Through anemones and enemynomes,
he ventures out with his crew.
It would be my greatest honor now
to present them all to you!"

Cosmo looked at me as if an anemone had sprouted from the top of my head.

"You're being weird," he said calmly, and moved on to reading the back of the conditioner bottle.

Strange, eccentric, oddball Cosmo had just called *me* weird? Had I broken my little brother?

What surprised me even more is that the thought made me so sad. Here's the thing: I had just wanted to get rid of some stupid stuff. I hadn't wanted to *change* Cosmo. Sure, he was basically a tiny, living, breathing embodiment of everything irritating.

But little brothers are annoying. They have annoying quirks and bad singing voices and dumb stories they repeat over and over and over, and you *think* you want them to stop all of that, but you don't. A person can't just be the good parts. For a person to be a person, you have to allow them to have an east and a west and a south too. Without the annoying parts, something vital, some true north, is lost.

I think I might have made things go from bad to worse, I realized.

Which, as you know, is what a character always says in a story right before things go from "worse" to "darker than you could ever imagine."

CHAPTER EIGHTEEN

✳

The Black Hole Who (Accidentally) Ate a Dog

The reason it went from worse to the absolute worst was that I thought it would be a good idea to play fetch with A Dog of No Name while Larry was around. It was warm outside, and Mom and Cosmo were at the dentist, so the pet crew and I were in the backyard getting some fresh air. I had a baseball the dog loved running after. I'd toss it and toss it, over and over, and she'd fetch.

That is, until the wind picked up, and the ball veered far to the left.

"Oh no," I said.

Oh yes, said the meddlesome wind.

The ball was there, and then it was not—disappeared entirely into the darkness of everyone's favorite black hole. The minute the ball disappeared Larry and I both froze and looked, wide-eyed, at the dog.

"Easy does it," I said, putting up my hands as if we were in the middle of a tense Western gunfight at high noon. "Let's not do anything crazy here. No sudden movements. We can figure this out."

Nobody moved. Time seemed to turn to taffy, stretching out and slowing down. I looked at the dog. Larry looked at me. We shifted our eyes again and again until . . .

"Noooooooooo!

"Waaaaaaaaaait!

"Doooooooog of Nooooo Naaaaaame!!!" I shouted.

But it was too late.

The dog had seen the ball.

The dog wanted the ball.

And the dog followed the ball right into a black hole.

✳ ✳ ✳

"Okay," I said. "Okay, okay, okay."

I paced back and forth along the length of the backyard.

"The key is STAY CALM and DON'T PANIC!" I said, panicking.

Larry looked at me as if he had an idea. He walked over to Mom's garden, leaned over a row of flowers, and started sniffing.

"We don't have time to smell the flowers, Larry," I said.

But he just kept doing it and doing it, until finally he reared back with an AAAA—AAAA . . . But alas, the CHOO never came. Bless his heart: My black hole had been trying to sneeze out our dog.

We made a list together of things we could try:

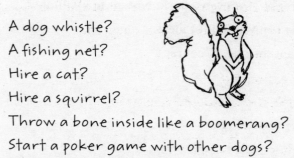

A dog whistle?
A fishing net?
Hire a cat?
Hire a squirrel?
Throw a bone inside like a boomerang?
Start a poker game with other dogs?
Get Larry to drink a gallon of soda and burp?

Suddenly Larry ducked behind a bush. I turned to see Skip the mail carrier delivering the mail.

"I always know it's good weather," I said, trying to distract him, "when you're wearing those cool shorts."

I was lying. The shorts were not cool. But Skip had given me an idea. Not a good one, mind you, but I was desperate.

"Maybe," I whispered to Larry, "I could tie a rope around the mailman, and dangle him inside you until the dog starts chasing him, and then pull them both out?"

"Step aside, kid," said Skip, "I've got important work. Do you think these CouponPalooza flyers just deliver themselves?"

After Skip left I tried yelling into the abyss of Larry.

"Dog of No Name!" I called. "Come back! We all miss you and think you're very intelligent, even when you run into the glass door to the patio over and over again!"

No reply. Not even a bark. Not even a whimper.

I was running out of ideas.

Except for one, of course.

CHAPTER NINETEEN

✳

Spaghettification

But who has gone inside a black hole?

Nobody, that's who.

Not one single person on this planet has been inside a black hole, seen what's there, and come back to tell us about it.

Was it like an afternoon the color of empty? A pie filled with alone? A map drawn to travel the lands of Bleak, Blank, and Devoid?

The science books say if you go into a black hole, and you cross over the edge called the Event Horizon, then your body will be stretched out. It's called "spaghettification" (sometimes referred to as the noodle effect).

And maybe, I thought, not only do you get spaghet-tified, but you also get to *eat* spaghetti. Plates of it. Piles of it. Mountains of spaghetti covered in sauce.

"It snows Parmesan cheese flakes inside a black hole!" I'd tell everyone at NASA when I got back. "The spaghetti is cooked al dente.

"I learned to juggle meatballs too!" I'd say.

Because who has gone inside a black hole?

Nobody, that's who.

Nobody but me.

CHAPTER TWENTY

✳

The Black Hole
Who Ate . . .
Me

Hello?

Hellooooooooooooooooooooooooo

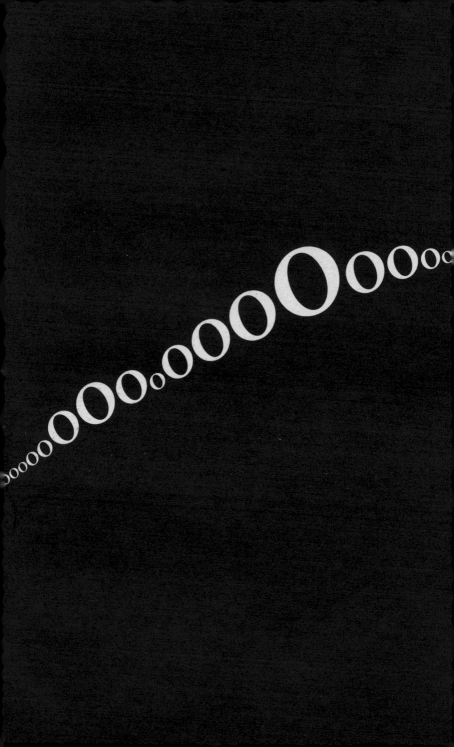

Ack!

Hello? Anyone there?

I seemed to be floating. The only thing that kept me from total and complete panic was the rope made of bedsheets I had tied around my waist. It was attached, back home, to the foot of our claw-foot tub, which was, I figured, the heaviest thing in our house. Cosmo had been using the tub when I'd left.

I'd double knotted the corner of a sheet around the tub's foot.

"This is fun," said Cosmo. "What are we playing?"

"Cosmo," I said, "whatever you do, don't untie this."

"Obviously," he replied.

"Okay . . . well," I said, "I guess this is good-bye. Here, take this."

I handed him a walkie-talkie.

"Ooh, cool, a wonky-tonky," said Cosmo.

As you know, ever since he could speak he had called walkie-talkies wonky-tonkies. No amount of convincing would sway him.

"Cosmo," I said, "think about it. You *walk* and *talk* using this contraption, not *wonk* and *tonk* . . . You know what, never mind! We don't have time for this conversation again. The world is turning upside down! The Dog of No Name was devoured by—"

I stopped myself. "Never mind! Just read the soap!" I yelled, racing out of the room.

After securing the sheets I'd gone to find Larry, but discovered he'd followed me and was standing right outside the door. Jumping into the black hole hadn't been that hard, really. He'd grown much larger than me. All it took was a running start and a complete loss of my senses.

So there I was, hanging in the depths of the black hole, the only thing keeping me from what I assumed was imminent death being the sheet tied around my waist. Was it possible that it was even darker than dark? A special kind of dark manufactured at a special dark-making factory out of gloom and bad dreams? It was dark like midnight hiding in the bottom of a drawer. Dark like Vampire Barbie's dream house. Dark like a shadow's soul, like a gutter's gutter. Dark like *DARK: The Memoir of a Seed*.

I looked down at the walkie-talkie attached to my belt. Could it possibly work?

I lifted it and pressed the button. "Cosmo? Are you there? Pick up if you are. Over."

No answer.

"Cosmo? Mom? Larry . . . ?" I tried. *"Anyone?"*

Leaving the device with Cosmo had been a last-ditch security measure at best anyhow. I had no illusions there would be any talking or walking inside a black hole.

But along with the walkie-talkie my backpack held several other things:

A flashlight

A rope

Snacks

A bear whistle

A compass

A watch

A notebook and pen

Most of it seemed ridiculous now. A bear whistle? For what? To scare away all the space bears? A notebook to write down all the scientific discoveries like "Day 1: STILL VERY DARK."

While I was floating there, I also made a mental list of all the things I did *not* bring with me into the black hole:

Bravery

A map

An inkling of a clue as to where I was or what was going to happen

A way out

Know what I started thinking about then? A book you read to me before bed when I was very little. Everyone knows the story: Alice chases a white rabbit with a pocketwatch down a hole, and ends up in Wonderland.

She gets lost. She has a tea party. A cat smiles a lot. She meets some playing cards. Blah, blah, blah. In the end she makes it home safely. I think we were supposed to wonder if it was all just Alice's dream, which is, in my opinion, a very uncreative ending for a book.

But this was different. I had gone down the rabbit hole, but I had a feeling there were no tea parties in my future.

No smiling cats. No playing cards.

And this was definitely not a dream.

✳

CHAPTER TWENTY-ONE

The Black Hole Who Snacked on a Tub

And then, out of that darkest dark came a voice.

A real voice!

"Stella?"

I pressed the button on the walkie-talkie and shouted, "Cosmo?! Can you really hear me? You need to get out of the tub and get Mom!"

"Where . . . where are you?" said Cosmo. "I'm scared."

"I'm not really sure where I am," I replied. "Are you still in the tub?"

"Yeah," he answered, "I'm still in the tub. But it's really dark. And I think there was an earthquake maybe."

"Well, turn on the bathroom light," I said. "There was not an earthquake because we don't live near the meeting of any tectonic plates. What are they even teaching you in school? Never mind. Look, can you please, please, please just get Mom?"

"I don't think I can."

"Cosmo," I said through gritted teeth, "I don't have time for this. I don't even know where I am. But I need to get some help, and—ack! Something touched me!"

"SOMETHING TOUCHED ME TOO!" yelled Cosmo.

During the yelling, my hand slipped and I lost the walkie-talkie.

"Noooooo," I said into the nothing.

Maybe Cosmo would still get Mom. And then Mom would get . . .

"What happened?!" yelled Cosmo.

But . . . how? How had I heard him?

Panicked, I fished around in my backpack until I gripped the flashlight. When I turned it on, it made an arc of light.

I tried to breathe, to stay calm. I couldn't see anything, so I used my hand to grope around in front of me.

"Ah!" I shouted. I felt something cold, and a little wet. Gross.

"Ow," said a voice.

"What in the world . . ." I replied.

"Stella," said a voice. "Stella, come in. Are you there? Something in the bathroom just touched me in the dark! Over and out? Stella?"

I swung my flashlight down until it illuminated one white claw. Then another. Then finally an entire tub with one shivering little brother inside.

"Stella!" said Cosmo. "What happened? Where are we?"

He was sitting in *our* tub. He was sitting in our tub *inside* the black hole.

"Oh no, oh no, oh no," I said, closing my eyes.

The black hole had actually pulled an entire clawfoot bathtub and a five-year-old inside? And what did that even mean? We were floating now, untethered to anything back in the world. What would happen to us? We would just keep floating forever, I supposed, like the Voyager Golden Record. Waiting, waiting, waiting for someone or something to find us. The Extraterrestrial Coast Guard, perhaps. The difference, though, was that the Golden Record contained all the greatest sounds of human history, and all I contained were eleven years' worth of loneliness, sadness, and a few good memories dropped in like the rarest of whale songs.

"Stella," said Cosmo. "Stella. Hey, Stella. Stella . . ."

"What," I asked, my throat tight with fear.

"I know you always say no to this, but, um . . ." He put out his little hand. "Would you like to get in the tub with me?"

CHAPTER TWENTY-TWO

∗

Larry to the "Rescue"

And so I got into the now-waterless tub with my soggy little brother, and tried to think of a plan.

"Where *are* we?" asked Cosmo. He was clutching my arm, clearly totally freaked out. I couldn't blame him. I was barely holding it together myself.

"I feel like we're in that book where they get swallowed by a sea monster," said Cosmo.

"Uh-huh," I replied.

"You know, I always thought they could have gotten out by just asking the monster," said Cosmo. "Politely, of course."

"Wait a minute," I said. "That actually gives me an idea. Just go with it, even if it seems weird. I'm going to say something, and then we're going to yell it together, as loud as we can. Okay?"

"Okay," said Cosmo.

"Larry, can you hear me? It's Stella," I said.

"LARRY, CAN YOU HEAR ME? IT'S STELLA!" we shouted.

No reply. I'm not sure what I'd been expecting. That Larry had learned to talk since swallowing me?

"Larry, if you can hear me, bounce up and down," I tried.

"LARRY, IF YOU CAN HEAR ME, BOUNCE UP AND DOWN!" we shouted together.

This time, something happened. It felt as if we were on water and the waves were slowly bobbing, making the tub rise and fall.

"It's working!" I said. "Okay, um, now let's yell: 'Larry, swallow some lamps.'"

"LARRY, SWALLOW SOME LAMPS!" we yelled.

A moment later something hit Cosmo in the face. I aimed my flashlight and peeled the book of stamps from his forehead.

"LAMPS!" we shouted. "NOT STAMPS. LAMPS! SWALLOW LIGHT. LIGHT!"

A moment later we saw a kite sail by in our flashlight beam.

"How about we say, 'Swallow sunshine,'" I suggested. "Nothing rhymes with that."

"Twine. Swine. Pine," said Cosmo.

"Sunbeam?" I asked.

"Scream. Team. Stream," said Cosmo.

"Well, what do you suggest?" I asked.

"I have no idea what we're doing, or where we are, but why don't we just yell 'HELP!'?"

So we did. We yelled "HELP" over and over, until finally, Larry must have understood. I'm still not sure what he did—whether he swallowed the actual sun or every lightbulb he could find—but suddenly we were flooded with light.

"Thank goodness for trained black holes," I said.

"THANK GOODNESS FOR TRAINED BLACK HOLES!" shouted Cosmo.

"You can stop yelling now," I said.

"Stella?" asked Cosmo. "I don't mean to be nosy, but who exactly is Larry?"

I wasn't sure what to say, so I tried one of Mom's tactics.

"Well," I said, "who do *you* think Larry is?"

"Uh, like, God maybe?" replied Cosmo. "But like, a Greek god. The kind that interacts with people a lot.

Answers questions. Makes stuff fall from the sky. Turns people into birds."

"Larry is, as far as I can tell, a black hole," I said. "He followed me home one night from NASA. I trained him. I fed him things. Problems mostly. Then the world started to fall apart. Then he accidentally ate A Dog of No Name. So I went in to fix everything, but in the process pulled our bathtub, and you, inside."

Cosmo looked at me, his eyes narrowed like when he's processing something.

And then, finally:

"Well, okay," he said. "It's an adventure, then. To save our dog. And our house. And your life. No problem. I'm happy to be ship's captain."

"I'm obviously the captain," I said.

"Okay, I'll be first mate," said Cosmo.

"Skipper," I replied.

"Second mate?"

"Regular mate."

"Deck hand?"

"Grateful passenger."

"Deal," said Cosmo.

"Deal," I replied.

And so, with just enough light to see directly ahead, and our stations assigned, we set forth on the maiden voyage of *The Clawfoot*.

CHAPTER TWENTY-THREE

✴

The Voyage of *The Clawfoot*

My first order of business as the captain of *The Claw-foot* was to figure out a way to steer our ship. Luckily, our lack of luck in staying tethered to home meant we had a wealth of bedsheets at our disposal. I had Cosmo help me, and together we attached them to the shower-head pipe, creating a makeshift sail.

"What about wind?" asked Cosmo.

"LARRY," I yelled, "WE NEED SOME WIND!"

"WIND," Cosmo and I shouted in unison. "WIND, WIND, WIND!"

For once, Larry must have heard us correctly, and had gone and swallowed a strong gust or gale or cyclone. It did the trick.

"It's working!" shouted Cosmo.

By turning the pipe and sails, we were able to do a decent job of steering as the tub floated through the nothing. Time passed slowly, and with no destination the desolation started to feel a bit like I was going crazy. So crazy, in fact, that at a certain point I could have sworn I heard music playing.

But not just any music.

"Hey, Cosmo," I asked eventually, "I know it's probably just in my head, but do you hear that? It sounds like raptor nails on a chalkboard. Like a thousand out-of-tune trumpets being played by tone-deaf monkeys. Like a marching band of broken instruments caught in a tornado. It sounds like—"

"My Fuzzles record!" cheered Cosmo, who had started to dance around in the tub. "How did I forget about these? You'll love this song. It's called 'Fartbreak Hotel.'"

Well, since those beans have left me, I found a new place that smells. Down at the end of Smelly Street, it's Fartbreak Hotel!

A Saturn-looking planet had a ring around it, but the ring was actually—help us all!—a giant record playing the soundtrack to my nightmare. We had pulled close enough that I could see the grooves of Cosmo's giant vinyl record, and the music had grown so loud that not even Cosmo was enjoying it any longer. I covered my ears, but to no avail.

Oh, I been so gassy, baby. Yeah, I been so gassy, baby.

"Normally I love this song," shouted Cosmo. "But this is just too loud. It ruins the subtle beauty of the lyrics."

"I don't even understand how it's spinning," I told Cosmo.

"Another thing that doesn't make sense," replied Cosmo, "is that smell. Do you smell that?"

"I do," I said, sniffing the air. "It's like a litter box full of sewer gas and inside are a wet dog covered in sauerkraut and an onion-eating skunk, both arguing over a stink bug that smells like elephant farts and old cabbage."

"Yes." Cosmo nodded, fanning the air toward his nose like a master stinkologist. "And also . . ."

"And also," I continued, "like if you were in a chicken coop with an old octopus who is performing a puppet show with his favorite dirty gym socks."

"Exactly," said Cosmo.

"You know what it really smells like?" I said. "This old class hamster we used to have. But he went . . ."

And then I remembered exactly where that hamster had gone. Exactly who had eaten it, and where we were now.

From somewhere below we heard a piercing, growling howl. It could only have come from someone cranky as a storm cloud and big as a space yak. Cosmo and I both looked over the side of the tub to see what was making the noise. And there, running on the record as if it were a giant hamster wheel, was none other than—

"Stinky Stu?!" I asked. "Is that really you?"

Stinky Stu, like all hamsters, had absolutely no idea what his name was. Or that we'd ever met. Or, I think, that he was a hamster at all. But one thing was for sure: Stu had changed. And by *changed*, I mean grown into a giant-bigfoot-mutant-hamster-monster.

We tried to think of a way to get closer and investigate the situation. And we tried our best not to inhale Stu's nauseating Eau de Hamster parfum.

"Hello, Stuart," I said. "You seem well. Have you been . . . working out?"

Stu looked up and grimaced. He kept running, and so the record kept playing. The wind seemed determined to push

us closer and closer, and I noticed that the closer we got to Stinky Stu, the less he was growling. Maybe he recognized me.

"I don't think he's dangerous," I said, my superpower acting up again. "I think maybe he's just kind of scared."

I felt bad. I was supposed to change Stu's woodchips every day and give him fresh water. Nowhere on the class pet care sheet did it list "allow hamster to be eaten by a black hole and dumped into cosmic Narnia."

"We need to save him," I said finally. "It's the right thing to do."

"Well, it's definitely the smelliest thing we can do," said Cosmo, "that's for sure."

Nonetheless, I had an idea.

"Larry," I yelled, "swallow some cheese! CHEESE!" I explained to Cosmo, "Stinky Stu really likes sunflower seeds and cheese. I feel like we have a better chance of calming and luring him with some food."

We watched Stu running on the record and waited.

"Does cheese make noise?" asked Cosmo.

"Not that I recall," I replied. "Why?"

"Because I'm starting to hear a sort of buzzing sound. Kind of a swarmy, buzzing sound . . ."

There, out of the dark, we saw what was making the noise: bees. Lots of bees. They were dodging and diving around us, circling like a bull around a matador, waiting to attack.

"CHEESE! NOT BEES!" I shouted to Larry.

But it was too late, of course. Stinky Stu had noticed the bees as well, and I could see the panic in his eyes. Before we could do anything about it, Stu turned and leaped toward us, his front paws latching on to the side of the tub.

"He's afraid of the bees!" yelled Cosmo.

What else could we do? We grabbed his furry paws and hauled him into the tub like a man overboard at sea. Once inside, Stu cowered on one side of the tub while Cosmo and I huddled on the other end. Thankfully, the bees had moved on.

"What now?" asked Cosmo.

"Now," I said, looking in Stinky Stu's direction, "we try to find our dog and a way home. And most importantly, we breathe through our mouths."

CHAPTER TWENTY-FOUR

✳

Captain's Log

I've decided to keep a Captain's Log. For scientific purposes, of course. If you are reading this, there is a good chance that—DON'T PANIC!—you are also inside a black hole. Welcome, friend!

CAPTAIN'S LOG
Day 2

Today we got our first scrap of a hint as to A Dog of No Name's whereabouts. We came upon a floating baseball, followed by a floating slipper, and later a floating newspaper. They were all chewed to shreds, and they were all going in the same direction. A distinct trail. Hope abounds!

Day 3

We've eaten all the sandwiches and fruit I packed. I'm beginning to worry a tad about the food situation. Well, at least we have my emergency bags of trail mix.

Day 4

Someone ate all the emergency trail mix.
(Stu. It was Stu.)

Day 5

The food problem has been solved. So, remember how I hated, loathed, despised, detested, and scorned Brussels sprouts, so I fed them to my pet black hole? And then remember how I got that puppy, and it went into the black hole, and I went in to rescue it, and now I'm trapped inside in a tub with my brother and a giant hamster? Well, turns out the Brussels sprouts are here too! Hooray!

They came at us in a green meteor shower, and when it was over, we had a tub full of Brussels sprouts. A lifetime supply, I think.

Let's just say that in the case of *Eating Sprouts vs. Starving*, it was a narrow win for sprouts, believe me.

Day 6

Very sick of Brussels sprouts.

Day 7

I am turning into a Brussels sprout.

Day 8

I think I may have a cabin fever of 104 degrees, but I'm starting to really come around on the Brussels sprouts!

Day 9

All hail the mighty Brussels sprout! Long live King Sprout! Bow down to his resplendent green majesty! I have even composed a song about Brussels sprouts!

Oh Brussels sprouts!
I wanna shouts!
You're like moldy green moss
that normally I would toss,
but I love you, I honestly love you.
I wanna hold you close,
you mini cabbage full of gross.

Oh, sprouts of Brussel!
I wanna nuzzle!
Taste like the inside of a shoe,
like a monkey at the zoo,
but I love you, I honestly love you.
I wanna hold you near,
fill my taste buds full of fear.

Day 10

Out of dire boredom, we've decided to embark on the task of deciphering what we are calling "Hamster Tongue"—the language of giant mutant hamsters throughout the universe.

Here is what we have so far:

GRAAAAAAAWRR! ..... Me like you.

GARUMPH! .... Me hate you.

AROOOOOOOGA! .... Me want ears scratched.

ARGH ARGH ARGH! .... Me rip your arm off if
you touch my ears.

RARRARRRARRAR! .... Me sleepy. Me want
lullaby. Sing me Brussels
sprouts song.

Day 11

A day of brilliant scientific discovery!

As anyone who has ever met him knows, Stinky Stu has an ever-so-slight problem with odors. He was our class pet, but we'd never been able to pinpoint the origin of the scent. Was it physical or, perhaps, spiritual? Well, spending days on end with him in a confined space, I have finally been able to figure it out.

I was deep asleep last night when I was awakened by a horrible smell, far more pungent than usual. I didn't even know a bad smell could wake someone up, but yes, apparently if it's bad enough, your brain starts shouting that death must be imminent because it smells like something else has clearly already died.

And there, in front of my face, was giant Stinky Stu, burping in his sleep.

"Can't . . . breathe . . ." I said, clawing my way over to the other side of the tub and gasping for air. "Death . . . by burping."

So that was it. The big mystery was solved. I reasoned that Stinky Stu had been so small in his original hamster form that we hadn't been able to see or hear that he was burping. It would probably have been pretty adorable back then, like a mouse with the hiccups, except in this case there was the smell. With his size upgrade, his gas output had increased as well, and unfortunately, also his burp speed, aggression, and scent.

Science and history take note: I, Stella Rodriguez, single-handedly solved the mystery of Stinky Stu's stankiness.

CHAPTER TWENTY-FIVE

✳

The Galactic Garbage UFO

Sadly, I was forced to give up on my Captain's Log, as 1) I ran out of paper and 2) Stinky Stu ate my pen.

We had also made the decision to no longer yell our wishes at Larry. We came to this after an unfortunate incident involving a request for good snacks and ensuing squid attacks. Onward and upward!

Today we ventured deeper into uncharted black hole territory. (Though all black hole territory is unmapped and unmoored, this section felt particularly rural.) It reminded me of times when I couldn't get to sleep at night, so I'd just lie there, eyes open to the dark, wondering if it had been minutes or if, perhaps, I'd been lying there forever. In those times, once my eyes adjusted, shapes of furniture would appear, barely recognizable and some-how unfamiliar. Now, in the black hole dark, I longed for the nothing to take the shape of *anything*—a bureau, a chest of drawers, a car, a . . . pile of garbage.

Yes, just when I thought I'd go mad from the noth-ingness, there appeared in the distance what could only be described as a great drifting glob of rubbish, odds, and ends.

"How'd all that garbage get here?" asked Cosmo.

As we sailed closer, I noted that much in the garbage pile looked familiar. There were larger items—hibachi grills, yard furniture, and lawn mowers that I recog-nized as the ones Larry had eaten during his rampage through the neighborhood. There was also garbage I recognized from our house: empty boxes of cereal, brands of soap or toothpaste we used, a mostly eaten roast chicken with the little potatoes, and beet salad that nobody particularly liked. There were vacuum bags, a broken umbrella, plastic forks, piles of dryer lint, a few hole-ridden socks, egg cartons, a chipped blue mug, piles of newspaper. I know this is going to sound strange, but looking at all that rubbish, I actually started to feel a longing inside. Sometimes life can get so confusing and unfamiliar that even a mound of what had clearly once been Mom's half-eaten waffles can make you feel a little bit homesick.

"I may have kinda, sorta fed a few things to the black hole back home," I told Cosmo. "Mostly garbage, clearly."

That's what I said, but what I thought was: *Had I actually thrown all this stuff inside? Surely there weren't this many things I wanted to get rid of in my life.*

As we got closer to the garbage barge, I attempted to navigate our ship around sinister tofu wedges and moldy bread. I zagged around evil-looking tests with bad grades, dirty laundry, and a sharp-edged photo of me from when I got the worst haircut in the world. It seemed as if everything here, everything I'd thrown into the black hole, had been changed into a wild, unpredictable version of what it once was.

Soon, a herd of left shoes was coming straight at us, and to avoid it, I had to steer perilously close to the pile. That's when I noticed there seemed to be some kind of door in the rubbish. And that the rubbish heap had a certain shape—a familiar one that I'd seen in movies.

"I think it's a UFO," I said to Cosmo and Stu, pointing at the junk.

We sailed past a window of the craft, and I tried to

peer inside. Were there alien life-forms native only to gravity-sucking space phenomena? Or—and I worried this would be the case—something far more threatening created by an object I had carelessly thrown inside the black hole?

"Get down!" I shouted to Cosmo and Stu. "I saw movement inside. Something colorful bopping about. Bright red, and blue, and yellow. They looked like party hats."

Had I thrown party hats inside Larry? I frantically tried to remember.

While our heads were down in hiding, *The Clawfoot* and the wind decided together that it would be a good time to lodge us in with all the junk that comprised the UFO.

"We have become one," said Cosmo, "with your garbage."

CHAPTER TWENTY-SIX

✳

The Not-So-Triumphant Return
of Storm Neptunian

And so we did the only thing we could: We climbed over garbage from our old world, and entered the unknown through the UFO's door (and by door, I mean an old stack of collapsed cardboard boxes I'd been too lazy to bring out to the curb back home).

"I think it would be helpful," said Cosmo, "to know what else you threw into this black hole."

"Well, I could make a list," I replied, "but it's not what went in that seems to matter. It's what things became. I mean, Stinky Stu used to be a quiet little hamster . . ."

We both looked over at Stu, who had just taken a very noisy bite out of the wall.

Suddenly we heard a sound coming down the corridor of the UFO. Footsteps, lots of them.

"Quick," I said to Cosmo and Stu, "over here."

We ducked behind an old, moldy shower curtain.

The footsteps marched closer and closer, until around the corner came . . .

"Gnomes?" whispered Cosmo.

We watched as a row of garden gnomes—ceramic, small, and inexplicably moving—made their way down the corridor. Left foot, right foot, with looks of determination on their faces.

"That's definitely a gnome," whispered Cosmo. "Gnome, gnome, gnome, Storm Neptunian, gnome . . ."

"What did you just say?" I asked.

"That gnome," replied Cosmo. "I know his name. How do I know his name? I guess maybe that's not his name. Hmm. But I wonder. HEY, STORM NEPTUNIAN!"

I tried to cover his mouth, but it was too late. All the garden gnomes turned toward the sound. The largest one in front motioned to Storm Neptunian, who in turn walked over and pulled aside the shower curtain.

"Storm Neptunian, good to see you," I said to the still toy-sized but now mobile nuisance.

"I'm not Storm Neptunian," he replied. "I'm a gnome. I love grass. Lawns. Colorful, pointy hats. All things related to garden gnome culture."

"First of all," I replied, looking down at what used to be my brother's toy, "you're wearing flippers and there's a snorkel attached to the side of your face. Second of all, that is not a pointy gnome hat on your head. That's . . ."

"A toilet paper roll," offered Cosmo helpfully.

"What's the mission of this craft?" I asked.

"Grass," replied Storm. "Lawn. Seeds. Gardening."

"Must be hard in space," I said.

"True," replied Storm.

"What with no dirt and no seeds anywhere," I said.

"Also true," said Storm.

"And since you're a scuba diver," I continued.

"Very true," said Storm. "Hey wait! I didn't mean to say that! You tricked me."

"So what's your name if it's not Storm Neptunian?" asked Cosmo.

"My name," said Storm, straightening his back and

his toilet paper roll, "is White Beard. We," he continued, "are gardening space pirate gnomes."

"Okay, what's *his* name?" I asked, pointing to another white-bearded gnome figurine.

"Also White Beard," replied Storm.

"And him?" asked Cosmo.

"White Beard," said Storm.

"Him?"

"White Beard."

"That guy?"

"White Beard."

"Over there?"

"White Beard."

"In the back?"

"White Beard."

"The leader up front?"

"Whitest Beard," said Storm.

"I can't believe I'm asking this of a tub toy," I said, "but please, take us to your leader."

CHAPTER TWENTY-SEVEN

✳

A Puzzle Called Home

We were brought to the front of the line, which wasn't very long, because gnomes really aren't that large. There stood Whitest Beard. His beard was, if anything, an eighth of an inch longer than the rest, but who was I to split hairs? (Get it? I may have become a bit delirious from the garbage fumes.)

"Captain Whitest Beard," I said, curtseying. I wasn't sure of the correct way to address a gnome. "Our ship, *The Clawfoot*, seems to have become, uh, lodged into the garbage on the side of your vessel."

"Gar blimey!" said Whitest Beard. He had a very high-pitched voice like somebody who'd inhaled helium.

"Well, we were hoping you could help us get on our way," I said. "We're trying to find our dog. You haven't seen a dog in these parts, have you?"

"OH THE HORROR! THE HOOOOOOOORROR!"
a small gnome voice came from behind us. We ran back
to see what the commotion was about, and found one
gnome cradling another who had clearly been about to
faint.

"*What's* a horror?" I asked.

"The dog! THE DOG! She came in the night. She . . .
she . . . SHE PEED ON US!"

"Oh," I said, relaxing at the news. "I mean, she's a
dog. And you're lawn ornaments. It's not that unusual
really."

"OH THE HORROR!" shouted all the gnomes again.

I rolled my eyes. But then rejoiced: They had seen
her! Even if it was from an unflattering angle.

"Galley-ho," said the captain. "You may sleep here tonight. But you pay the toll tomorrow. Then we will help
you dislodge from our ship," he said.

"Oh, thank you—" But he cut me off.

"And if you hornswoggle me," he said, "then by dislodge I mean we will throw you each into space!"

"Well, shiver me timbers," I said, wondering if I'd
break my toe by kicking a ceramic gnome.

Later that night, while walking to my ship quarters,
I saw that Storm Neptunian's door was open a crack.
I was about to say hello when I noticed that he was

looking down sadly and petting something. I angled so that I could peer one eye through the crack of the door, and saw that he was holding none other than his Storm Neptunian scuba helmet.

"Storm Neptunian misses his home too," I explained to Cosmo and Stinky Stu back in our room. "I'm pretty sure we can convince him to come with us."

"Why would we want to do that?" asked a sleepy Cosmo.

"B-because . . . well . . ." I stammered, realizing it would be entirely too hard to explain to Cosmo my theory: that bringing his Storm Neptunian toy with us in the tub would jog Cosmo's memory, and make him turn back into his old, annoying self.

That night, lying in my gnome-ship bed, I thought about that word. *Home.* What does it even mean, really?

The gnomes probably longed for the lawn in our neighborhood back in the real world. A patch of sunny grass, with Mrs. Nimbus gardening nearby and a cat pouncing on real and make-believe intruders. To them home might mean the sound of frogs and crickets on summer nights, and the feel of brief morning showers during which the statues would have tipped their heads back if only they could.

And what about Storm Neptunian? Was this spaceship really what felt like home to him? No, his home was the place where he could wear his helmet as he descended down, down, down into the sea, where the turquoise turned to navy blue, where the flecks of mica glittered like stars in the darkness, where schools of fish changed direction like wind. His home was the smoothness of algae, the roughness of coral, the closeness of a whale passing above like a cloud, first blocking the sun, then moving on to reveal its light again.

For me, the question was harder.

I knew, at least, what my home was not. My home was not an upside-down world where nicknames, and scars, and brothers' true personalities could disappear. My home was not a bathtub. My home was not in the depths of the blackest black hole.

So what was it then?

Was it like the crossword puzzles you used to love? In the puzzle called "Home" would clues lead me to the answers? Bedroom. Kitchen. Garage. Swings. Table. Fresh. Baked. Cookies.

Maybe home was more like a locket—a thing you kept close, and could share if you wanted, or could keep as your own secret.

Or maybe it was more like the soles of old, beloved shoes, the middle of the sofa cushion, a worn path, a discolored poster, a cup ring on an old oak table. Something you see every day, and perhaps take for granted.

I decided then that home was probably all of these things: something sought after, found, held close, used, well-worn, and best of all, familiar.

CHAPTER TWENTY-EIGHT

✶

The Escape

"Cosmo, wake up," I whispered to him in the dark.

I had tried for hours after bedtime to think of a plan. Maybe we could give the gnomes some bedsheets as payment? Some Brussels sprouts? While I'd become somewhat attached to them on the trip, I wasn't sure Whitest Beard would see their value.

So, in the end, the only plan I was able to come up with was a cowardly, middle-of-the-night, here-goes-nothing escape. I had to do something. All those thoughts of home had reminded me that ours was in shambles, memories were missing, and our mother was probably sick with worry.

"What? What's happening?" asked Cosmo, rubbing

the sleep from his eyes. "Are they throwing us into space now? Do I have time to use the bathroom?"

"Just get dressed, get Stinky Stu, and meet me at *The Clawfoot*. There's something I have to do before we leave."

I felt my way down the long, garbage-lined hallway in the dark.

"So gross," I said, touching what was either a pile of wet yarn or wet brains.

When I finally reached Storm Neptunian's room, I slowly creaked the door open. By the tiny light of his scuba helmet, I could see he was asleep. Which went perfectly with my plan to, well . . .

"Kidnap?" asked Cosmo when I got back to the boat. "The thing you had to do was kidnap Storm Neptunian?"

Muffled noises came from the pillowcase under my arm. The small scuba toy inside was struggling like a particularly upset housecat, and it was all I could do to keep him from escaping.

"Come on now," I said to Cosmo. "Start digging. We need to get *The Clawfoot* free and get out of here before the gnomes wake up."

That, however, was going to prove pretty impossible once Storm Neptunian started sounding the Scuba Team Alarm on his suit. It was high-pitched and extremely irritating, and I remembered it clearly from when Cosmo would play with it in the tub back home.

"Help!" shouted Storm. "I'm being gnome-napped!"

I managed to find the OFF button, but every time I hit it, Storm would just wait a few seconds, then hit it again. Finally, exasperated, I just dropped him in the tub.

"You'll do hard time for this!" he shouted.

With the help of Stinky Stu and Cosmo, I was able to dig out most of *The Clawfoot* by the time we heard the small, creepy ceramic footsteps approaching.

"Get in!" I shouted.

We all jumped into the tub, and I immediately began force-feeding Brussels sprouts to Stu, hoping for a miracle in the form of a supersonic belch. Luck must have been on our side that night, because after just a few handfuls, Stu let out the biggest, most disgusting, powerful, ship-shaking burp in the history of burps. It caused such force that it pushed us away from the UFO just as the gnome horde reached the door.

"So long, Bimphy!" I shouted. "Take it easy, Dafoodle! Don't forget to write, Fudgewick! I shall miss you most of all, Loopglynn, Toodles, and Zoomwinkle! Stay beautiful, Nickelbells! Give my regards to Broadway, Pimpert!"

As we sailed away at the Speed of Burp, Storm Neptunian turned off his alarm and sat, sulking, on his throne of sprouts. Cosmo went over, put his hand on Storm Neptunian's, and tried to be of some comfort.

"There, there. I don't know why my sister kidnapped you, but I'm sure she had her reasons. Do you like Brussels sprouts?"

Storm Neptunian looked around the tub, then at Cosmo, then down at his helmet.

"Something about this place feels very familiar," he said.

"Well of course," said Cosmo. "We took a bath in here together every day since we met. Wait a minute. Is that true?"

Cosmo looked over at me, then Storm. "I remember," he said in awe.

"I . . . I . . ." stammered Storm. "I remember too."

I can't believe I'm about to admit this, but as Cosmo hugged his stupid scuba doll, I actually started to tear up a little. Even worse, when Cosmo took him in his arms and held him on the prow of the ship like a wooden mermaid, I actually started to sing along.

Through anemones and enemynomes,
he ventures out with his crew.
It would be my greatest honor now
to present them all to you!

It was nice, I have to say, to have my brother acting like himself again. And I realized that for Storm Neptunian, the ocean wasn't actually home. For him, it was Cosmo, his truest companion, his tide that pulled him in and out and the one who rode with him on the backs of seahorses and dragons.

In the distance, I saw a small light, much like a star. It reminded me of the night-light in my room back home, and without a better plan, I steered the tub to go toward it. I must say that just then, with Cosmo and Storm Neptunian singing, and the small lighthouse of hope in the distance, the tub felt, for a moment, a bit like *my* true home.

CHAPTER TWENTY-NINE

*

Flat Giraffes and
Cardboard Moons

While Cosmo and Storm Neptunian played, Stinky Stu and I used Stu's stomach gas and our sheet sail to navigate our way toward the beacon in the distance. The closer we got, the larger *it* got, until we finally realized it was no light at all, but rather an entire planet.

"I think we should get closer and explore," said Cosmo.

"I second that," said Storm Neptunian.

"Stu," I said to the hamster, "do you by any chance have an opinion to add to that of a tub toy and a child?"

Stu looked at me, wondering, I assume, if maybe now would be the right time to eat me.

I tried to maneuver close enough to get a good view of the planet without actually touching down and putting us in harm's way. There were trees and lakes, some fields, some rivers, but nothing seemed to be moving. On top of that, I had this eerie, creeping feeling that I'd been here before. But how? That made no sense. I think I would have remembered if I'd been to a planet inside a black hole at some point in my life.

"Hey look," said Cosmo. "There's some kind of moon-looking thing over there."

Sure enough, approaching on our left was a crescent moon.

"And it's attached to the planet by some kind of wire," he continued.

We sailed slowly past the moon, and saw that not only was it attached to the planet by what seemed to be an extremely long piece of stiff wire, but it was also made out of cardboard.

"It's brown," I said. "And made of paper. It looks like something someone at school would make."

We kept looking down, searching for more signs of life. Finally, in the distance, we saw a herd of some kind of animal. We maneuvered toward them.

"Looks like safari animals," said Cosmo.

Which was true, sure, but there was something off about these too.

"Ack!" I yelled.

One of the giraffes had turned, and when it did, it all but disappeared.

"It's flat," said Cosmo. "Hey, Stella, can giraffes be made out of construction paper?"

"Well," I said, "they can if they were made by a kid, then put into a black hole, and then transformed into a living thing."

It had, by then, finally dawned on me why the planet felt so familiar. The paper river below, the crookedly cut stars, the flat animals with poorly drawn mouths and eyes—it was *Stellarium*, the planet you and I had made so that I could join the science club, the one that I had, of course, thrown into the black hole with the other memories.

I remembered so clearly the day we made it. I remembered the decision to use wires to attach a moon and stars and clouds. The clouds were cotton balls. The stars were cardboard painted gold. And then we'd run out of gold.

"And look there," said Cosmo, "up ahead are some orange and red and yellow stars. They're so beautiful."

"And down through these clouds," I said lowering the ship a little, "is a river made of old book pages."

"Whoa," said Cosmo, "how do you know that?"

"Because," I replied, pointing to the river, "this is my planet."

CHAPTER THIRTY

✳

The River of Words

Cosmo and the others were asleep. We'd decided to stay above the planet for the night and try to figure out any potential danger before landing. I had volunteered for first watch.

Currently we were hovering above the River of Words that you and I had made. It had started as a dumb story I wrote when I was Cosmo's age, and I hated it, so I wanted to throw it out. But then you had the idea to cut up the words and make the river out of them. You said it was where a person could go fishing for new ideas and whole new sentences.

I fished for one now. "This sentence is made like a

wasp's nest, out of spit and wood pulp chewed up by the queen," I announced.

Nobody was awake to listen.

I liked the idea of sentence-fishing. It was like the opposite of the day I thought the black hole was going to eat the world. I silently fished for more.

This sentence was constructed out of the hundreds of trees that grow every year simply because squirrels forget where they buried their acorns.

This sentence is soggy and unreadable from being left in the tub too long.

This sentence will be shredded and used to line a hamster cage.

This sentence was launched into space and will pass within 1.6 light-years of the star Gliese 445 in about 40,000 years.

Does this sentence smell okay? Its expiration date has passed.

This sentence was torn from a notebook that lists all the different kinds of light: underwater, and looking up through leaves, and illuminating a new detail on the face of someone you know by heart.

This sentence is still half heartless and half grown.

This sentence smells like sweet dying flowers.

This sentence went extinct due to lack of belief in its existence.

This sentence just says you are gone.

You are gone.

But every time I read it, it makes no sense.

I try to fish for a new word to put at the end, something like "here" or "just at work" or "but going to walk through the door any minute and say 'Oh, hello, Sweet Pea.'"

But my line is twisted and my lure has escaped.

This sentence believes we ruin things if we try to make them last forever.

This sentence is really a map, which is really a memory, which is really a wish to go home.

CHAPTER THIRTY-ONE

✳

Stellarium

Once we decided it was safe to land—the biggest threat we could see being flat giraffes—we resolved to set *The Clawfoot* down on Stellarium.

"To the north is the Lake of No Fish," I explained to our crew, pointing. "So named because I hate fish. One touched me during a camp swimming trip. I mean, it turned out to be a piece of seaweed, but still. The horror.

"To the south," I continued, "is the Volcano Pequeño."

"Small volcano?" asked Cosmo, looking toward the peak of the extremely large crater of the volcano in the distance.

"It was a lot smaller on the model," I explained. "On

top is an observatory to look at the stars. That was Dad's idea."

"But what if the volcano erupts?" asked Cosmo.

"We felt stargazing could use the added excitement," I replied. "And to the east," I continued, "we have the Hills of Hysteria, which we decided is a place where you could laugh, and the laugh would keep echoing off the peaks and valleys forever. And of course where we are now must be the west, because we're at the banks of the River of Words. Which way should we go? Should we vote?" I asked.

"Or," said Storm Neptunian, "we could just ask whoever *that* is."

He was looking south. A figure was moving toward us over the land made of papier-mâché junk mail and glue. Was it another flat animal? A rhino perhaps? A large jungle cat with paper teeth?

"It looks like an elephant with two trunks," said Cosmo.

"Or an octopus with only two tentacles," said Storm Neptunian.

"Well, think," said Cosmo. "What else did you put on Stellarium when you made this place? An emu with two snakes attacking its head?"

"Um, no," I said. "Not that I can recall."

The closer the figure came, the more I realized it

wasn't a creature at all. It looked as if someone had taken several spools of yarn, planted them in a garden like seeds, and waited to see what kind of creature might grow. The one that had was all sorts of colors, and seemed to be nothing more than a torso and arms. It wore flower leis around its wrists and ankles.

"Are you going to sacrifice us to a volcano?" Cosmo asked it. "If so, take me."

"No!" Storm Neptunian shouted. "Take me. I couldn't bear to go on adventures without you."

"No, me," said Cosmo.

Cosmo and Storm Neptunian stared at each other, long-lost cheeseballs finally reunited. The strange yarn-being slapped its arm over the spot where its head would be if it had one.

"Look, trust me," it said. "If we had a volcano filled with something other than glitter, I'd *gladly* throw you *both* inside. Sadly, we do not, so you'll just have to follow me."

* * *

"We're a Tribe of Sweaters," the creatures explained. "This is our planet. It's called—"

"Stellarium," I interrupted.

"GASP. How did you know that?" asked the lead sweater.

"Listen here, Zip-Up Sweater and the Button-Down Gang," I said. "This is so *not* your planet. It's mine. And so are you, actually. Our aunt Celeste made you, and you somehow ended up inside this black hole on this planet."

"BLASPHEMY!" shouted the sweaters. "HERESY! SACRILEGE! HOW DARE SHE DISRESPECT THE MIGHTY STELLA?!"

"The who-za whatta?" I asked.

"Here on Stellarium," replied the lead sweater, "we worship the Great Stella."

"But she's—" started Cosmo, pointing at me. I cut him off before he could finish.

"And you *like* this Stella?" I asked. "You don't want to knit her up into yarn prison or anything like that?"

"Oh, we *love* Stella," said the sweaters, making some kind of weird *S* gesture with their arms. "We would do anything for Stella. We revere her. We worship her."

Before I could ask more, a conch-shell horn began sounding.

"It's time!" shouted the sweaters. "It's time!"

They all ran toward the volcano, prancing and clapping. I finally caught up to one of them.

"Time for what?" I asked.

"Time for the reading of *The Book of Stella*," he said excitedly.

"What is that? Like a holiday or something?" I asked.

"No," he said. "We have a reading once every hour on the hour. It's the best. Stella is so wise. Stella is a genius. We marvel at her every word."

I blushed, and touched my hair nervously. "Well, I don't know if I'd say *genius*," I started to say, but stopped short. I stared at the sweater at the top of some kind of book-shaped shrine. In his sleeves was a very distinct, very bright blue book with white stars on the cover.

"Is that . . ." I asked, horrified. "My *DIARY*?"

✦

CHAPTER THIRTY-TWO

A Reading from
The Book of Stella

May the tenth, 1976," read the sweater. "I, Stella Rodriguez, am officially in love."

"Oh no," I said. "No, no, no."

"Tony Luna is, by far, the dreamiest boy in the entire school," continued the scratchy mothball of a sweater. "And he's in the science club, which means when we get

married, we can totally work at NASA together and eat lunch and make out on our breaks and—"

"Stop!" I shouted. "Stop the reading."

I climbed up the shrine steps, and attempted to grab the diary, *my* diary, from the savage sweater. Before I could grab hold, two of his henchsweaters grabbed me and tangled me up in their arms.

"You don't understand," I said. "That's my diary. I'm Stella. *The* Stella, the one who wrote those extremely personal, some would say mildly embarrassing, things."

The sweater tribe all stopped their chattering and stared at me.

"Why have you come here?" asked the reader sweater. "Why have you come here, telling these lies?"

"First of all," I said, "they're not lies. Second of all, we're trying to find our dog and our way home. Have you seen a dog? Kinda small, sorta . . . partially trained?"

"She means she barks at her own tail," added Cosmo.

"And what is this dog's name?" asked the sweater.

"Well, she doesn't exactly have a name . . ." I tried to explain.

"There is no mention of a nameless dog in *The Book of Stella*," he said suspiciously, holding up the diary. The crowd nodded and began chattering again. They had all, apparently, memorized my diary. Good grief.

"It's true," I said, "that there is no mention of a dog in

my—*The Book of Stella*. That's because I stopped writing in it before we got the dog. Look, have you seen a dog on Stellarium or not? Because if not, you can save us a lot of time and we'll be on our way and you can continue your society formed around my diary."

The sweater turned like he was looking over the valley in wise contemplation.

"We may know of such a dog," he said.

"Wait, really? Where?" I asked.

"You claim to be the Stella," said the sweater. "Prove it."

"I didn't bring my school ID," I said, "because, you know, we're in a black hole and I didn't think I'd be needing it."

"The entry I was reading," said the sweater. "Tell us what the rest of it says."

"Seriously?" I asked.

"Seriously," said the obnoxious, not to mention nosy, atrociously argyle sweater.

I sighed loudly, and closed my eyes to block out some of the blisteringly bright embarrassment.

"It says I have—I mean *had*—a huge, honking, super-mega crush on Tony Luna and . . . maybe sorta kinda goes on to describe our future wedding and how many kids we'll have and what their names will be. There! Are you happy now?"

"Tell us about this wedding," said the sweater.

I tried to lunge toward him and strangle him, but his lack of neck was a major hindrance.

"Fine, fine," said the sweater. "You know much of the book. However, there is one passage I have never shared with the other Stellarians. The very last passage. I was saving it, for what I do not know. Until now. If you can tell me what the passage says, I will believe that you are the Stella."

I paused. I looked at Cosmo. Of course I knew what was in the last entry in the diary. It was from well after the last day I could remember when I cared about diary things like pop quizzes and the slight-but-mostly-imaginary mustache of Tony Luna. It was the entry that made me feed the whole silly diary to Larry in the first place.

So here was my choice. Door number one: I could pretend I had no idea what the entry said, and never have to say the words out loud. Certainly preferable. Except for the part about desperately wanting to find our dog and go home. So that just left the choice behind door number two: I could tell them what the entry said. I could say it out loud for the first time ever, even to myself.

No thanks, is what I wanted to say to that.

But what I actually said was:

"The last entry was about my dad, our dad," I said,

motioning to Cosmo. "It doesn't say it, but he died." I paused for a moment, then continued. "The day I wrote that entry, I was trying to remember if my dad had a moon-shaped birthmark on his right hand or his left hand. And I couldn't remember. And I panicked. So I went and got my diary, which I hadn't written in for months since he'd been gone. And I made a list. I listed everything about him I could think of, every little thing that I was afraid I would forget. It took me almost all day and even some time after supper.

"And later, when I got rid of all my memories in the black hole, I thought I'd forget everything on the list. But I haven't. I know that the first thing on the list is how everything he cooked was a little burnt, but we were all too nice to say anything. And how he called me kiddo, and how much I missed the way he called me kiddo. And how he smiled when I was telling a story. And how he held his coffee mug. And how he always used these weird sayings that nobody understood. Like, 'Have you been drinking muddy water?'"

When I said that, Cosmo laughed.

"He said it when I sat in front of the TV and blocked the view," said Cosmo, smiling.

"And it says what his favorite song was, and his bad dance moves, and how he sang in the shower. It lists his best jokes, and his worst jokes, and how he always lost his glasses. It even says what his shadow looked like, very tall next to mine when we were walking together.

"The list was my own Voyager Golden Record, sent from me *that day* to me in the future. I wanted her to remember."

I looked at Cosmo, who looked back, tearful but still smiling.

I looked over at the sweaters—all bowing their neck holes toward me.

I looked up at the paper moon and paper stars above me, the ones I had built with you. A beautiful, flawed, shining world we had made together, one I stood on now.

"He's gone," I said, "and there's a hole in my life."

The sweater holding my diary handed it to me.

"I'm sorry I doubted you," he said. "I believe this is yours."

And then he added the most wonderful words:

"Now we will show you the way to your Dog of No Name."

CHAPTER THIRTY-THREE

✳

To the Singularity

At the center of any black hole lies something called a *singularity*.

The word *singularity* means a point where some property is infinite. In the center of a black hole, for example, there is a gravitational singularity, a point that contains a huge mass in an infinitely small space. Here, gravity becomes infinite, and space-time curves infinitely, and the laws of physics as we know them cease to operate.

I read that back when I was doing my black hole research, back when I gave Larry his name, short for Singularity. I thought about it again when the Sweater Society told us where our dog might be hiding.

"If you follow that glitter star up there," the leader said, "you'll be going true north. In that direction, a day's journey, there is a place. It has a great darkness, a great gravity, and the closer you get, the more it will draw you near."

The sweaters helped load us back into our tub.

"Thank you," I replied.

And I have to admit, I meant it. I had hated those sweaters forever back home, but they, like so many other things I tried to get rid of in the black hole, were something it turned out I needed. Those ugly sweaters had gotten me to say something out loud that I'd been avoiding for a long time—something that Mom, and Cosmo, and the school therapist hadn't been able to get me to admit: that you were gone. I thought it would feel bad. But in truth, it actually made me feel just a little bit lighter.

We set our sails in *The Clawfoot*, and with some help from the sweaters and the wind, took off from Stellarium back into the dark sky.

We sailed over the River of Words, over nouns and

adjectives and a few verbs splashing up at us with a wave. We watched in the distance as the volcano spewed a burst of baking soda and glitter. We passed a long, slender tree that had once been a small branch.

"I'd almost forgotten about that," I said. "We used a small wisp of a tree branch and stuck it in the north of the planet. To give it guidance like a compass, that's what Dad said. And at the end, we attached that star up there."

"That *stella* up there," said Cosmo, knowing well the meaning of my name.

Cosmo and I and our faithful companions looked at the star, glittering among the cotton ball clouds, pointing us true north. I felt, for the first time, that maybe, just maybe, we were headed in the right direction.

CHAPTER THIRTY-FOUR

✳

A Hamburger on a Ferris Wheel

The trip from Stellarium took longer than a day, I'll tell you that. Sweaters! They're ugly, scratchy, and they have no concept of time.

While Cosmo and I were in the middle of our 109th game of Brussels sprouts checkers—a favorite game, second only to "How hard can I fling this Brussels sprout at you before it hurts?"—we spotted some objects below the starboard bow of our vessel. Or maybe it was the stern. The port? Look, it's a bathtub. The point is, we saw something.

"Maybe it's a way to call for help," said Cosmo.

"Maybe it's something to eat," I said.

"Grumple grumphmar," said Stu.

Trouble was, the one direction we couldn't steer our ship was down. So, after much deliberation, we decided that one of us would have to go down by sheet rope and check things out. Stu was eliminated due to obesity (the Brussels sprout diet was doing absolutely nothing for his figure), Storm couldn't climb in flippers, and I was ship captain with all the responsibilities that it entails, so Cosmo was left as the clear choice.

After we hauled Cosmo back up, he seemed much calmer than I'd expected. In fact, he almost seemed a little sad.

"Cosmo?" I asked. "You okay? What was out there?"

His face was pale as the moon, and he refused to meet my eyes. Wordlessly, he handed me the things he'd fetched out of the depths of space.

"Oh," I said. "Your drawings. I wonder, um, how those got here . . ."

Cosmo folded his arms over his chest, went to the far end of the tub, and sat with his back to me. Storm Neptunian, always the free thinker, decided that if Cosmo was mad at me, then he was too. Even the hamster turned his hairy back to me. Great.

"Cosmo, let me explain," I tried.

"You hate Brussels sprouts!" yelled Cosmo.

"True . . ." I said.

"And Aunt Celeste's haunted sweaters. And garbage night, and the musical genius of the Fuzzles. And sometimes . . . I think you hate *me*."

"Hate *you*?" I asked, honestly stunned. "I don't hate you. That artwork got eaten accidentally, I swear. Larry would eat every new picture you gave me. I mean, I love these drawings. Look at this one," I said, holding one up. "What is that? A giraffe, um, kissing an angry llama in a pool of macaroni and cheese? That's art."

"It's me and Storm Neptunian," said Cosmo.

I turned the picture upside down.

"Oh yeah," I said. "I see that now."

I wondered why the drawing hadn't grown or morphed like everything else. I didn't get to wonder for long, though. As Cosmo explained what the drawing actually was, it seemed to wake up from a space slumber. The images on the page unwound—lines of marker and crayon peeling up and able to move, dance, and swim freely on the paper.

"Whoa," said Cosmo. "Did I make that happen?"

"Now look at this one," I said, holding up the next drawing. "Wow. A hamburger on a Ferris wheel? What's not to like?"

"That's Stu on his wheel in his cage."

"Yeah, I knew that," I said. "I was just kidding."

The drawing of Stu on the page began racing around in circles.

Cosmo craned his neck, just a bit, to see which drawing was next.

"Is this one two Bigfoots having a laser gun fight?" I asked.

"It's Mom and Aunt Celeste wearing sweaters and having tea."

"Teacups!" I said. "Of course. Who drinks laser guns?"

Cosmo climbed over Stu, who was also paying attention now to the moving pictures.

"And that's you," said Cosmo, pointing to the next drawing.

"Am I a superhero there?" I asked. The figure in the drawing was wearing a red cape and holding either a brontosaurus or a car over her head. The cape began blowing in a breeze on the page.

"Yeah," said Cosmo. "One with super strength. And that's you *and* me," he said of the next piece of art.

He'd drawn us somewhere in the neon-green grass, with A Dog of No Name lying down nearby. He and I were kicking a soccer ball, and we were smiling, and the sun was wearing sunglasses and smiling too.

The thing was, I had never played soccer with my brother. Not once.

To be honest I couldn't remember the last time I had played anything with him at all.

"These are all so good," I said. "You have pictures of almost everyone. I was thinking, we should do one of Dad too."

"Dad?" said Cosmo. "I thought I wasn't allowed to talk about him with you."

I wanted to tell my brother he was wrong, except I couldn't, because he wasn't. Just recently if he had mentioned you, I would have gotten upset and just fed more things to Larry. I would have kept trying to get rid of everything bad in my life until there was nothing good left either.

"Well, did you know that Dad once ate a dog bone?" I asked. "His best friend dared him to when he was your age, and he did it."

"No way," said Cosmo, his eyes wide.

"Way," I replied. "And did you know that he could burp the alphabet? And that one time he let me call a psychic hotline? And did you ever hear that the way he met Mom was that they were total strangers sitting next to each other in a movie theater, and she fell asleep with her head on his shoulder? And he didn't say anything. He didn't wake her up until the credits. Until the *end* of the credits."

"Well, did *you* know," said Cosmo, "that Dad and I had the same favorite animal? It's a baby duck. And he said if I want when I'm sixteen I can change my name to my favorite: Ralph. And also sometimes we ate cookie dough after school and you weren't there."

I smiled. Because of the ducks. And Ralph. But mostly because you had let *me* eat cookie dough too, when Mom and Cosmo weren't home. And I realized how much I missed you. And how much Cosmo missed you. And how much Cosmo needed me. And how much I needed him right back.

And so we talked about everything that we remembered. We talked about big days and small days. We talked until it felt as if you were there, almost, or at least until the part of you that was in Cosmo, and the part of you that was in me, were both shining so brightly it didn't seem like there was any dark left in the black hole at all.

CHAPTER THIRTY-FIVE

✳

The Memory Keeper

It was a nice moment until suddenly, from the drawing of the two of us with our dog, there came a loud woof as the picture scampered around in excitement.

"Hey, it barked!" said Cosmo.

And then, out of the distance, came another bark in answer—much, much louder. It echoed and continued as if it was an infinite thing.

"Did you hear that?" asked Storm Neptunian. "Toys and dogs never get along."

"It's just the drawing," said Cosmo.

"I don't think that was the picture," I said.

The two dogs continued barking and howling back and forth like in a quiet neighborhood at night.

Ruff-ruff

Arooooooo

Ruff-ruff

Arooooooo

We followed the sound.

Finally, we reached a place where the scant light in the black hole seemed to swirl around, and in the center there was the darkest of dark spots. The singularity. There, sitting in a giant cardboard box, was none other than . . . A DOG OF NO NAME!

We raced *The Clawfoot* toward her until we were close enough to pet her. She stared up at us with her dopey dog-grin.

"Hey, girl," I said, scratching behind her ears. "We've been searching everywhere for you. And in this case, that is totally not an exaggeration."

Our dog looked momentarily concerned when she saw Stu, but I petted the giant hamster's paw to show her all was well. Stu showed his giant teeth in what I like to think was a smile.

"Look," said Cosmo.

Behind our dog in the makeshift nest of a cardboard box was a pile of things. As we looked closer, I realized it was the rest of the memories I had boxed up back home and tried to throw away and forget. She'd collected them, and protected them. Probably, I thought, they reminded her of home.

"Dad's red hat!" said Cosmo.

I picked it up and placed it on his head.

"Very dashing. Very adventurous," I said.

I looked at the other items in the pile. They were all exactly the same. They hadn't morphed into anything scary. Cosmo and I lifted each one from the pile. We inspected everything closely—the rock polisher, the head lamp, the chemistry set, the periodic table, the bug collection, the model of the human brain, the book about astronauts. They all seemed exactly as they were when you and I had used them.

Our dog gave a whimper. The whimper, like the bark, went on and on into the darkness.

I petted her behind the ears the way she liked.

"You must have been so lonely," I told her. "I'm sorry that I let you accidentally get eaten by a black hole. I'm sorry I called you kind of dumb. And I'm mostly sorry I never gave you a name." I paused. "I guess I was scared that if I gave you a name, I'd start to care about you. And if I cared about you, what if something happened to you?"

After a moment of consideration, I told the dog, "I'm going to call you Sagan. After Carl Sagan, of course, the astronomer who chose all the items for the Voyager Golden Record. You, like him, were infinitely wise to have collected all these memories for us."

I looked at the pile again. I picked up the framed photo of you, the one that I had gotten so angry at Larry for eating. There you were, still opening your telescope, still laughing and happy. I handed it to Cosmo, and he looked at it too, and he smiled. It was a good picture, after all. It would always be a good picture. The memory would be the same forever. It wouldn't change and it wouldn't morph into anything scary. I knew then that none of my memories of you ever would. They were mine for always, a safe place to go when I felt sad or scared, lonely or lost.

I put my arm around Cosmo. He put his arm around me. Sagan licked both our hands. I closed my eyes, feeling a point of infinite love and infinite grief, and comfort in knowing, for the first time, that I have infinite space inside for both.

CHAPTER THIRTY-SIX

★

A Recording, Part One

There was one last item in Sagan the dog's pile. Cosmo lifted it and inspected it closely.

"Isn't this your old tape recorder?" he asked. "And there's a tape inside. Can I play it?"

"It's a recording I made with Dad," I said.

Now it was Cosmo's turn to look thoughtful. He hovered his finger over the PLAY button.

"So, can I?" he asked.

I nodded.

Cosmo pressed PLAY.

But we didn't hear a sound. None at all. Instead, quite unexpectedly, the door to our house appeared.

What I mean is, we were still in the tub, and still in

the black hole, but in front of us was the door to our house with its chipped green paint, the one that led to our kitchen.

"Is that . . . our door?" asked Cosmo.

"Yes. No. Uh," I said, feeling as if my brain had become a Brussels sprout. "Actually, I have no idea what's going on at all."

The tape recorder in Cosmo's hands whirred. Then, through the thick silence, I thought I could hear matching muffled sounds from beyond the door.

I leaned out of the tub and, with the tips of my fingers, gingerly pushed the door open, then pulled my hand back quickly. The door *creeeeeaked* open slow and spooky-like, and we all arched our necks in fear and curiosity to see what was inside.

"It looks like a pitch-black tunnel," said Cosmo. "Like a waterslide or something."

"I don't want to go on that waterslide," said Storm Neptunian. "I do not think it ends in splishy-splashy fun."

"No, now, just wait a minute," I said. "If it's a door and a tunnel, then I think I know what it is. I read about it. I think it might be something Einstein theorized."

"He had a theory about doors?" asked Cosmo.

"No," I replied. "About things called wormholes. They're basically these portals to get you from one place

in the universe to another. Like you enter one door, and
then seconds later you exit in another part of the galaxy.

Like a subway system that's providing amazing shortcuts. Sort of the way a worm can go in one side of an apple and exit the other side, instead of taking the long way around. Hence the name."

"So wait," said Cosmo. "If we go in that door, we might exit on the other side of the galaxy?"

"I don't know," I said. "But we currently live in a tub in a black hole, so what do we have to lose?"

I knew we had to go through the door. I started to have that feeling—you know the one. Like when you're the hider during hide-and-seek, and it's all peaceful crouched in the closet, the hems of coats around your ears, but you know *something is coming.*

One at a time we climbed to the edge of the tub, then across the threshold of the door—first my little brother and his tub toy, followed by a super-sized hamster, and then an infinite dog, and finally yours truly.

* * *

And then, after what felt like a faster-than-light descent down a dark slide, we were home.

Except we weren't.

Not exactly.

It looked like our kitchen, and it smelled like our

kitchen—some combination of dish soap and toaster waffles—but something was off. Something was different.

"The wallpaper," said Cosmo, pointing. "It changed back."

He was right. That was it. The wallpaper in this kitchen was the wallpaper we had in our house almost a year ago. It had vegetables on it, eggplants and carrots and things, and it existed in our kitchen before you even got sick.

The new wallpaper, from after you were gone, had utensils on it, faded silver spoons and forks that Mom said made her laugh. She had said she needed to laugh, and that she liked peeling off the long strips of paper.

In the Before, there were artichokes on the walls. In the After, you were gone, and the walls were covered with strange spoons.

"I think we're in the Before," I said to Cosmo.

Cosmo was young, sure, but he knew exactly what I meant. We had shorthand in our house. If someone said something was from "Before," we knew it meant before you died. I guess that's how time works. A bad thing happens, and it splits your life in two, into a Before and an After. There's really nothing you can do about it. Except it helps, I've realized, if you have people who share your same Before and After.

Cosmo was still holding the tape recorder. The recording would definitely be labeled with a capital *B* for *Before*. Suddenly, a voice began speaking on the tape, and when it did, the speaker appeared, right there in front of us. He looked a little like he'd stepped out of a faded photograph—not quite real, but not an illusion either.

The person was, of course, you.

And as the tape played back words, you began to speak.

CHAPTER THIRTY-SEVEN

✳

A Recording, Part Two

"Now here's a good one," you said. "How do you organize a space party?"

I stood there. I knew the memory well. In it, I was sitting in a chair at the kitchen table with you. But now, my chair was empty. Your question just hung in the air.

I looked at Cosmo, but it became clear that neither he nor anyone else could see what I could see. It was my memory, after all. Not sure what else to do, I slowly walked over to the chair and carefully sat down. You just continued smiling, sipping your coffee.

"Um," I said, "I don't know. How?"

"You *planet*," you replied with a slight smile.

"Plan it. Good one," I said, recalling my lines. "I've got one too. Uh, where do geneticists like to swim?"

"Where?" you asked.

"In the gene pool," I said.

"Ha! I like that one," you said. "Hey, by the way, have you heard about the new book about anti-gravity?"

"What about it?" I asked, my voice barely a whisper, my hands shaking.

"It's impossible to put down," you replied.

And we laughed. You laughed because of the joke, and I laughed because it was either that or burst into tears.

"How do you think like a proton?" I asked.

"How?" you said.

"You stay positive," I said. I couldn't giggle this time.

That one you liked. Big laugh for the proton.

"Why are chemists great at solving problems?" I asked.

"I don't know. Why?"

"Because they have all the solutions."

You laughed, then said, "Why can you never trust atoms?"

"Because they make up everything," I replied.

Whoops.

"Hey, you got it!" you said, still laughing.

Okay. Phew. I'd messed up my line, but it seemed okay.

"So, I guess you got your recording," you said. "I'm glad."

"It's definitely a big responsibility," I said, back on script.

"Oh, I agree," you agreed. "I mean, you choose someone with one of those high-pitched screaming laughs, and maybe the aliens turn around."

But I wasn't really paying attention. I was thinking about how me saying the wrong line earlier hadn't caused a cosmic rip through the fabric of space and time. *Could I change the script?* I wondered.

"Dad?" I said. "Can I tell you something?"

I waited for you to say your old line. The one about how if they put some weird snort-laugh on the Voyager record, we could say buh-bye to hovercraft cars and magical space cheese. So long secrets of the galaxy.

But instead, you said:

"Of course, sweet pea."

I paused. I'd imagined this moment many, many times, but now that it was here, I couldn't come up with anything that seemed important or worthy enough to say. So instead, I just said the truest thing I could think of.

"I miss you," I said. "I miss just talking to you."

"You can talk to me anytime," you said. "About anything."

"But not really," I replied.

"Why not?" you asked.

"Because," I said. "You're gone."

"Am I?" you asked. "Well, maybe tangibly, but how do you think I'm here right now? In this black hole of yours? It's not the physical me, no; it's the me that lives in there."

You pointed to my heart, which felt, I admit, as if it would collapse or burst at that moment.

"It's like the stars in our constellations that we made," you said. "Even if one star dies far, far away, its light is still visible, and the constellation it helped to make remains. A thing can be gone and still be your guide." He took my hand. "You know what I would say in any situation, what advice I would give, how much I'll always believe in you. That belongs to you. That love. And no one can touch it, or alter it, or take it away. It will live in you your whole life. Who knows, maybe longer."

And then, the things you were saying, they were no longer words, at least not ones that needed to be said out loud. They were coming from inside me. You were right: I did know the words you would say, and how you would say them, and where your voice would crack with laughter.

I reached over then and we hugged. And it didn't feel like just a memory or a ghost hug; it felt real. I pretended I was a tape recorder, and I made an effort to press every bit of this moment into my memory—the smell of your shirt, the scratch of your cheek, the feeling of being perfectly cherished and safe. If I were the Voyager, this moment would be the one I'd play for the aliens. *Look*, I'd say. *Look how beautiful our world can be.*

I wanted to stay there forever, but suddenly I heard the whir of tape, and then an abrupt click.

You sat back up straight in your chair. You took a sip of your coffee.

"Now here's a good one," you said. "How do you organize a space party?"

The recording. It had started back at the beginning. It wasn't very long, and would always end. That's when I knew. I could stay here, forever, lost in a memory. But that's not what you would have wanted. It's not, I realized, how I wanted to spend my life either.

I stood up from the table and walked over to Cosmo. He looked bewildered. He truly hadn't been able to see or hear the recording.

"Can I see that?" I asked.

He handed me the tape recorder. I looked down at the buttons. I knew which one I had to press.

I put my finger on STOP. Cosmo put his small finger

on top of mine. We held hands and paws with Sagan, and Stinky Stu, and Storm Neptunian.

"Ready?" I asked.

"Ready," said Cosmo.

It was time to go home.

CHAPTER THIRTY-EIGHT

*

Shades and Hues

Cosmo and I didn't speak for several minutes after the tape recorder clicked off. Who has ever lost something, and then been allowed to glimpse it again? Things finally made sense. I had to meet Larry, I had to throw my problems inside him, and I had to be forced to face them. I had to get to a place where I could hear your words, and let them in, and understand that you would always exist in me, even though you were gone.

"What are you thinking?" asked Cosmo finally.

"I'm thinking," I said, "that you were right about the Voyager. That it should include sad things along with the rest. I'm thinking that the story of Earth is not the sound of a tractor. It's love. And loss. And somehow finding the courage to love again.

"What are you thinking?" I asked Cosmo.

"I'm thinking," he said, "that we need to go through that door."

He pointed to the door in the far corner, the one that led to the rest of our house.

"Yes," I said. "I get the same feeling. I think the recording—the memory—became a portal. I think we can use it to travel back to our real house, present tense."

And so the four of us made our way across the kitchen, past the table where you no longer sat. When we reached the door that led to the rest of our house, I let everyone go before me.

I paused and looked at the door ahead. I had that feeling again, that things were changing. Every cell in my body was straining like a dog on a leash. Every hair on my arms was raised and tilting toward home. I wanted to get there, but leaving was so hard. It would be a truly long journey without you. But I had had this moment: a moment I could keep close, in the bottom of my pocket, and take out to warm me when all was dark and cold.

* * *

Once we reached the other side, the first thing I heard were Cosmo's cries.

"Where'd Stinky Stu go?! He was just here, and now he's gone!"

We looked around the living room, but a 400-pound hamster would be pretty hard to miss. Then, something started moving and squeaking at our feet.

"Stu!" said Cosmo, lifting the animal.

Rodent-sized Stu, smelling as bad as ever, hopped onto Cosmo's hand and nuzzled him. I had a feeling that when school started again, I would be bringing New Stu as the class pet. Stinky Stu, the first hamster to venture into a black hole, would be staying right here with us. It was only fair, after all. Once you live in a bathtub with someone, that someone really becomes part of the family.

While Sagan sniffed everything wildly, beyond excited to be home, Cosmo nervously pulled the string on his now-back-to-toy-form Storm Neptunian.

"Arrrr! Yo ho ho! Walk the plank, ye landlubbers!"

"It's actually kind of an improvement," I said, smiling.

Suddenly we heard a noise in the kitchen, behind the door we'd just come through. Were the memories still on the other side? Had we not made it home after all?

Slowly, slowly, we creaked open the door and peered our heads around the corner.

"Mom!" we both shouted.

Mom braced herself as the force of our surprise hug attack nearly knocked her over.

"Bug, Cosmo, hello," she said. "Oh my, to what do I owe the pleasure?"

"We just really, really, really missed you, Mom," I said, basking in the fact that she'd called me Bug. I touched my chin. My scar was back too. Maybe I'd call Tony Luna later. You know, just to make sure I was in the Test Tubes again.

"Yeah," said Cosmo. "Thanks for being our mom, Mom."

"Well," she said, flustered but smiling, "you're welcome. I've been calling for twenty minutes. Lunch is getting cold."

Twenty minutes? Cosmo and I looked at each other.

Lunch, which we both wolfed down, consisted of the

absolute best grilled cheese sandwiches and tomato soup in the universe.

"Hungry?" asked Mom, making us both second helpings.

"Like I've been eating Brussels sprouts for weeks," said Cosmo. We both busted out laughing.

Mom sighed, and smiled. I smiled right back.

"I never seem to know what anyone is talking about," said Mom. "But I will say, it makes me happy to see you two spending time together."

I couldn't help thinking the exact same thing. I guess other things had morphed and changed inside the black hole too. Changed for the better. I felt less alone, that was for sure. I realized how much my brother and I needed each other. I realized how much I took Mom for granted, and how much I missed her while we were gone. I guess that's what pain can do if you allow it: crack you open, let light in, and show you what's on the inside. Our adventure through the dark had shown me shades and hues of myself that I couldn't have otherwise seen. I guess more is always being revealed. And maybe, just maybe, you haven't taught me everything you have to teach me just yet.

CHAPTER THIRTY-NINE

✳

The Black Hole Who Saved Me

After eating as fast as I could, I ran to my room to find Larry, hoping he was okay. What if something had happened to him while we were inside, or when we'd crossed back over to the real world?

"Larry?" I called. "Are you here? Are you okay?"

When I opened the door, I couldn't help but gasp.

"Larry! You're . . . you're . . . HUGE!"

It was true. Larry had at least quadrupled in size, now towering over me and filling almost the entire room. I guess that's just what happens when you put an entire bathtub inside your pet black hole.

He moved around uncomfortably, trying to get close to me in his joy at having me back, but bumping and

✳ 189 ✳

absorbing the desk and chair, then brushing the top of himself on the ceiling constellations.

"I was worried about you," I told Larry. It was true. I hadn't realized how attached I'd become to my pet.

"Thanks for saving us," I said.

Larry looked down at me. He seemed to say, *Anytime, old friend*, and also, *Do you think the store sells this bedroom in the next size up? I seem to have put on some weight . . .*

As I looked up at him, into his strangely familiar galaxy-filled eyes, I wondered if Larry was perhaps full of more mysteries than I could ever know. I recalled once as a little girl looking inside the bell of a tulip. It was a sunny day, and the light through the petals gave everything a purple-red glow. It looked like a whole tiny galaxy in there, with the Aurora Borealis, a stamen moon, pollen-freckled stars, and perfect petals overlapping like layers of time. Maybe what I'd thought was my superpower was actually just this: I was finally able to see that nothing was simply good or bad, that everyone contained multitudes, and that I, like anyone, was a beautiful, swirling, chaotic galaxy of all the things that had ever happened to me.

How odd, I thought, *that it was a black hole who led me back from my own darkest dark*. Now it was time for me to do something for him, even though the very thought broke my heart.

And so, ignoring the screams of "WHERE ON EARTH IS OUR CLAW-FOOT TUB?!" that were coming from Mom in the bathroom, I prepared for one more good-bye.

CHAPTER FORTY

✳

The Black Hole Who Said Good-bye

This story ends on a morning the color of comets, with a girl dressed all in black. A girl who had grown. A girl with a hole by her side, and a good-bye on the horizon.

"My name is Stella Rodriguez," I told the guard at the gate to NASA. "I have an appointment."

"Yes, yes of course," said the guard, fumbling nervously with charts and a phone. His eyes darted from me to Larry and back, getting larger and larger each time.

Larry seemed pleased to be on an adventure. Stinky Stu, used as bait to lure Larry here just before dawn, yawned in my pocket, probably dreaming of sunflower seeds.

The nervous guard led us to a large room and left us

there alone. I looked around at the desks and the maps on the wall, hoping that someday, maybe, one of the desks might be mine.

Soon, a scientist joined us, the woman I had spoken to on the phone. The one who had promised that NASA would launch Larry back to space, where he could be released, and live where he belonged, happy and free.

"Do you really think that's what's best?" I had asked her.

"I do," she'd said.

Now she leaned down and looked right at me. She had kind, strong eyes. She spoke softly.

"You're a very brave girl. You've taken very good care of your friend. The universe is full of amazing things, but some aren't meant to stay with us forever."

"Can I ask you a question?" I said. "What is Larry? I mean, do you know? Did you make him at NASA or did he come from space? Is he a black hole or a wormhole or what?"

"We try not to label things too much here," said the woman.

"But hasn't NASA literally labeled every star in the sky?" I replied.

The woman laughed. She had a good laugh, a kind laugh. The kind that could go on a recording to the stars. You would have approved.

"I'll give you a moment to say your good-byes," she said. She smiled, touched my shoulder, and left the room.

After she had gone I turned to Larry, who was calmly eating a pile of expensive-looking microscopes. Outside, the dark had turned to early light. The scientist was right, I thought. Nothing could stay forever. We want to hold things, but the moon always melts into the morning.

"Hey Larry," I said. "Come here." The well-trained black hole did as he was told.

"This is the big day, huh? The day you go home. Isn't it exciting?" I asked. "I can just imagine."

I wondered what Larry felt about going home. I bet it felt like that moment between getting a gift and opening it; between writing a letter and sending it; that feeling at the edge of autumn, when there's electricity in the chilly air like a billion buzzing insects; when the very leaves on the trees are dreaming of setting off across the meadows and fields.

Larry looked at me, totally confused, but like he loved the sound of my voice just the same. I smiled, remembering the day I'd found him, shivering and cold in a box by the curb. Just a small black hole that came into my life out of the rain.

"You know," I said to Larry, my throat starting to feel tight. "Sometimes . . . well, sometimes what you think is a black hole in your life, sucking everything into its darkness . . . it turns out to actually be a wormhole. A portal. A way home. If you can keep on and face the darkness, it will, in the end, take you where you need to go. It will take you back to yourself. That's what you did for me."

I wanted so badly to just throw my arms around Larry and give him a giant hug. But instead, I approached slowly, and spread my arms carefully around the edges of the dark.

Larry's eyes grew wide. Was someone really embracing him? Touching him, finally, after so much time?

"It's okay," I said. "I won't disappear."

We both closed our eyes. It felt then, in that moment, as if I was wrapping my arms around every wonderful, heartbreaking thing: the smell of fresh-picked dandelions, Mom cooking in the kitchen, Cosmo's tiny hand in mine, memories, constellations, planets, the rushing of time, the slowing of time, and every memory in between. As I stood with my arms around Larry, I could have sworn I heard the faint, faraway sound of laughter. Your laughter.

The recording, I thought. *It's still inside.* But I realized it's not just your laughter. It's mine too. And when they launch Larry into space, the sound of the two of us laughing together will be there, always and infinitely among the stars. Just as we planned.

I finally understood. It turns out that it's possible, if you are careful, to feel all the feelings that come along with having and caring for a black hole, but to still not be consumed by it. I was, I realized, no longer afraid—not of this darkness, or any other.

They say that a black hole lives at the center of every galaxy. And I believe that now. There would always be a black hole at the center of me, of my galaxy, my life. But it's mine. It's part of me. I faced it. I trained it. I tamed it. And finally, I set it free.

There's a hole at the center, but that's okay, because it's full of such beautiful, beautiful things.

✦

Acknowledgments

This book is dedicated to my stepfather, Eddie, who raised me from a very young age, and who passed away two years ago. There comes a time in every life when one is followed home by a black hole, or is considering adopting one as a pet. (Please see the appendix of this book in either case.) It took me a long time to turn my own particular grief into something shaped a bit more like a book. This novel, and every book I've written or will write, would not exist without Eddie's words of unwavering encouragement. For that I am so very thankful.

Of course, there are always countless guides along the way, and I am deeply indebted to many. Thank you to Emily Van Beek for her wisdom, patience, and huge heart; Molly Jaffa and Sean Daily for believing my books should be shared farther and wider; Lauri Hornik for her endless encouragement on this and all adventures; Carly Massey and Jake Currie, who have read every draft of every book; Bobby Holub, who sits with me and hashes out stories for hours (which any writer knows is the most romantic thing in the world); Duane Lee for talking with me in my naiveté from the Shanghai Astronomical Observatory about black holes and wormholes; NASA for publishing an article about micro black holes a few years back that contained this inspirational line: *"Why, your neighbor could have a pet black hole and you wouldn't even know it"*; Carl Sagan for launching a message in a bottle to the stars; and finally to Indy: Thank you for climbing the stairs. This is not a metaphor. Indy is our dog, he's afraid of stairs, and my office is on the second floor. He makes the journey every day just to say, *"Keep going."*

✳

A BEGINNER'S GUIDE TO THE CARE AND FEEDING OF BLACK HOLES

written by
Stella Rodriguez

BLACK HOLES FOLLOW YOU HOME IN THE DARK. You can find them lots of places probably, but definitely check inside any cardboard boxes you left curbside by the garbage cans in the rain.

They will eat: flashlights, dust bunnies, your little brother's beautifully executed artwork, jars of pennies, infinite numbers of left shoes, hamsters, favorite photos of your dad, decks of cards, pencil erasers, one hundred and forty-seven garden gnomes, yard games, yard toys, hibachi grills, humming-bird feeders, hideous sweaters, Brussels sprouts, bags of trash, vinyl records, rock polishers, head lamps, chemistry sets, cracked beakers, periodic tables, models of the human brain, books about astronauts, red hats, baseballs, recordings of laughter, dogs, brothers, bathtubs, and you.

Black holes have complex digestive systems, so it's very important that they receive proper nutrition.

It is very dark inside a black hole—specifically, there is absolutely no light. Black holes should have access to a constant supply of light, which aids their emotional well-being by providing the necessary brightness and joy to help prevent health problems. Be kind. Compliment your black hole. Say nice things. Sing bright songs.

In addition to light, the basic diet of a black hole should consist of nothing living—no dogs, cats, hamsters, mice, or reptiles. Feeding small pets to your black hole should be avoided for obvious reasons, including hairballs.

Your pet may also enjoy treats. While many black holes enjoy stars and planets, they are starchy and should only be given sparingly as a treat. Other snacks your black hole might enjoy are lava lamps, glow sticks, disco balls, and sparklers on the Fourth of July.

Black holes are fragile animals that must be handled carefully. Do not allow small children to approach the black hole's event horizon unsupervised. To cuddle your pet, stretch your arms around the outside of the black hole's darkness. DO NOT actually enter the black hole, but instead, stay at the edges, where it is safe.

Black holes are (somewhat) trainable with patience and the lure of small, furry treats. They like to sleep in your bed. Sometimes you find a black hole staring up at the sky, seeming as if it wishes to go home. They get cranky when tired. They grow. They want. They'll run away if you yell at them. They need love like anything else.

Putting a thing inside a black hole does not necessarily mean said thing is gone forever. In fact, recent studies have shown that when something is thrown inside a black hole— say, something that annoys you, a problem you hate, or just something that makes you sad to look at it—well, that doesn't mean it disappears never to be seen again. The gravitational force will pull it inside, but then, the problem will grow. And morph. And change into a giant, wild, uncontrollable version of what it once was.

Be careful when you throw something bad inside your black hole. You may find you've gotten rid of the good as well.

Black holes are complex, beautiful creatures. They can take you to places inside and out-side yourself you never realized you needed to go. They can teach you about grief, loss, loyalty, and most of all, love. The infinite bond you make with a black hole, when nur-tured and grown, can last a lifetime. Maybe longer. So make sure you take good care of your pet black hole while you have it. Be pa-tient. Be kind. Hold it as close as you can, and let it know you are not afraid. And when the day finally comes to say good-bye, set it free, with love, into the infinite beyond.

✳